aHunter4Saken

By

Cynthia A Clement

Cover Design: RomCon- www.romcon.com
Cover Image: Jenn LeBlanc- Illustrated Romance

Dedication

To Linda

You loved the Hunters from the beginning.

Thank you for all of your help and support over the years.

Chapter 1

Niail awoke unsure of his mission or where he was. A shooting pain pierced his skull. If the loud hammering did not cease soon, he would go crazy. His stomach rolled and he tried to move. Something blocked him and refused to budge. He only knew one thing for certain; he was a Hunter, an elite warrior always in control and ready to protect.

"Easy." The voice was soft and female. "You took quite a hit on the head. Stay put."

"I need to use a basin." His words were barely audible, but within seconds a pail was handed to him.

"Here."

When he had emptied the contents of his stomach, he leaned back and groaned. He was in a bed and it had been sheets that had kept him from escaping. He tried to focus his eyes, but everything was blurred. It was easier to keep them shut.

"Where am I?"

"Blackfeet Reservation." A damp cloth wiped his face. "Bobby found you at the side of the road. It looks like you took quite a beating before someone threw you there."

"I do not remember."

"That's not surprising." There was a soft sigh. "You've got a concussion, a huge gash on your head, and so many cuts and bruises, it's a wonder you're alive."

"I have had worse." He rubbed the side of his head and frowned. At least he thought he had. If only the noise would stop.

"Take these."

Niail's head was lifted up and two tablets were put in his mouth. A glass was pressed to his lips. "Swallow. They'll help your headache."

Niail did as he was told and then his head was lowered to the pillow. "Thank you."

"Get some rest. I'll wake you in a couple of hours."

He didn't have the energy to argue. He let the world fade away, as the oblivion of sleep claimed him.

The next thing he knew, his head was being shaken back and forth. He grimaced as pain shot through his skull. Why couldn't they leave him in peace? He tried to ignore the shaking, but they were insistent.

"Wake up."

He opened his lids.

The most beautiful pair of dark brown eyes he had ever seen, stared down at him. There was concern in their depths. Something must be wrong. He struggled to get up, but his body refused to move.

"I've been trying to wake you for the last fifteen minutes." The eyes belonged to the voice from earlier. "I don't want you dying on me."

"Hunters are hard to kill." The words seemed to stick to his tongue.

"What were you hunting?" There was amusement in her tone. "Most things are out of season this time of year."

"I was not hunting."

"If you say so." A cool cloth wiped at his forehead. "It wouldn't do for you to be caught, though. It's illegal, unless you belong to the tribe."

Niail frowned. He still did not understand the double meaning of words in the English language. At least on Cygnus, there was only one meaning for each word. It made life simpler. He shifted, and pain shot up the back of his head. He bit back a groan. A Hunter handled pain. He did not let it control him.

"I can't give you anything else." There was regret in her voice. "Try and sleep."

Niail did not argue. Darkness dropped over his brain, quietening the throbbing ache behind his eyes.

The gentle voice continued to wake him at regular intervals. A couple of times she offered him medicine. He took it, but it did not relieve the hammering, or the static in his head. Everything was clouded and only sleep lessened his agony.

There was loud shouting when he opened his eyes for the first time on his own. The noise was enough to wake the dead. He groaned and pushed up onto his elbows. Sunlight streamed through the windows. It was time for him to leave.

The sheet fell away from his bare chest and a shiver of cold skittered across his body. A wave of weakness threatened to drop him back onto the pillow, but he fought it. He needed to find his unit.

"Wow. How did you get all those muscles?"

Niail's eyes narrowed. He turned toward the voice. A small boy of about five years old was leaning against the bed. He had a mop of short dark hair, and wide innocent eyes. He looked carefree and curious. Niail had always imagined a boy should look like that. It was the opposite of what he had been as a child.

"Mom said you were hurt. I don't see any bullet holes." The boy's voice held awe. "You look like a superhero and nothing can hurt them."

"What is a superhero?"

"Leave the man alone," a soft voice scolded. Niail turned his head to look at a young girl who stood near the door. She was about a year older than the boy. "Mom also said he needs for us to be quiet."

"Tell that to Uncle Jake." The boy jerked his head to the closed door. "He's been yelling for at least ten minutes now. I'm surprised you weren't awake earlier."

"Sleep makes my head feel better."

The boy pursed his lips. Niail did not think his answer had pleased him. Maybe the boy was having second thoughts about him being a superhero. Niail was at a loss. He had never been around children before.

"Were you near bad spirits?"

"I do not see spirits, good or bad." Niail pushed against the headboard and leaned his head back. The pain behind his eyes eased a fraction. "Are they supposed to help?"

"No." The little girl spoke now. "Bad spirits would weaken you. At least that's what Grandfather believes."

"Then I suppose I must have seen a whole lot of bad spirits last night."

Niail winced as the noise from the other room increased. Whatever they were fighting about it must be serious. Hunters did not argue, but over the last several months on earth, he had learned humans seemed to enjoy it.

"Can't you remember?" The boy leaned closer.

Niail shook his head. "It is a complete blank."

"That's why Mom had to keep waking you up last night." The girl ventured a few feet closer to the bed. "She said that you might have died."

"Then I owe her my life." Niail tried to remember what their mother looked like, but all he could recall was a gentle voice, and a beautiful pair of brown eyes. The same eyes stared back at him from the young boy beside him. "You have your mother's eyes."

"I have my Daddy's" The girl's voice held regret. "He left us."

Niail's gut tightened. He did not understand human men. They had no honor, or sense of duty. To abandon your woman and children was unforgivable. Niail turned his gaze to the little girl.

She was pretty, with the same dark hair as her brother. Her eyes were black. The same color as Hunter eyes and deep within them was the belief that she did not measure up. She was not much older than her brother, but life had taught her some cruel lessons. She was already halfway to becoming an adult.

"My eyes are the same color." Niail softened his gruff voice. "All Hunters have black eyes."

"What's a Hunter?" The girl took a step closer.

"We are an elite warrior race sworn to protect."

The girl's eyebrows rose. "You do good?"

"Yes."

"So you are a superhero." The boy jumped up and down. "I knew it. All superheroes have muscles."

"You also wear some of the sacred symbols." The girl pointed to his left arm. "That's why you were brought to Mommy. She knows about those things."

Niail looked at his arm. "You mean my campaigns?"

The girl nodded. "I'm going to learn about the Star People when I'm older."

Niail's head whirled for a second. They could not possibly know that he was not from Earth. He shut his eyes for a second and tried to concentrate on what he might have said while he was unconscious.

Darkness was all he remembered.

He tried to focus harder, but pain shot through his skull. Nausea rolled over him and still no memory of last night. His brain refused to function. He sighed. There was no point on dwelling on it now. He would deal with whatever he had said later.

"Are you okay?" The girl's voice was full of concern. "I can get my Mom."

"Best leave her." Niail opened his eyes. "What is your name?"

"Peta." She lifted her chin. "My grandmother has the same name."

"It is a beautiful name." Niail tried to smile. Humans liked smiling, but he had never understood why.

"My name is Wil. It's short for Eluwilussit."

"I am Niail."

"It sounds funny. Where are you from?" Wil leaned his arms on the bed.

"Far away." He hoped this would satisfy them.

They nodded. Just then the noise in the other room was punctuated by the slamming of a door. It echoed through to them and then silence. Niail heard the distinct sounds of crying. He struggled to fling his sheets back until he realized he only had briefs on. A quick search of the room did not turn up any of his clothes.

"What do you need?" Peta was now leaning against the bed like her brother.

"My clothes.

"My Mom had to wash them. They were very dirty and wet."

Wil bobbed his head up and down. "They stunk too."

Niail frowned. What had happened to him last night? He must have been on a mission. To have been ambushed and left at the side of the road was unheard of for a Hunter. To be alone on a dangerous mission was not logical. Nothing about his current predicament made sense.

The crying in the other room was replaced with the sound and smell of cooking. His stomach shifted uneasily. Food was the last thing he wanted. He needed to get his clothes and leave. Before he could move, the door opened.

"What are you two doing here?"

"Niail is awake." Peta ran to her mother. "He needs his clothes."

Niail's gaze lifted from Peta, and he focused on her mother. A sharp jolt of awareness shot through him and he gasped. The static in his head exploded, but when he inhaled, everything settled back in place. His brain might still be foggy, but he recognized immediately that there was something unique about the woman who had just walked into the room, and into his life.

"I had to wash them." Peta and her mother walked to the bed. "They're torn and need some mending. When I'm finished, I'll get them back to you."

"You do not need to fix them." Niail swallowed the lump in his throat. "I can sew."

"You're a man of many talents, but right now I don't think you would be able to concentrate long enough to hold a needle."

He could not argue with her.

Nothing was as usual.

The woman who stood in front of him was evidence of that. He felt her eyes touch him, almost caressing in their concern. Never had he been aware of a female before. This shook him to his very core. He was sworn to a life of honor and duty.

Women were not a part of his life.

He forced back the sensation of awareness and looked up at her. She was beautiful. Everything about her was perfect. She had dark black hair, deep brown eyes, luscious full lips, and a voluptuous figure. She was a woman a man would enjoy holding.

What the hell was he thinking?

Hunters did not embrace women.

He looked down at the bed and tried to ignore his body's reaction to the thought of touching the beauty before him. That hit on the head had done more damage than he had thought. He had forgotten his mission; next he would forget he was a warrior.

"You're still in pain." She let her finger drift over his forehead. "You need more sleep."

A shock of electricity shot through him. It took his breath away. He forced his heart beat to relax, and glanced up. She was frowning. Had he done something wrong? Trying to read humans was something he had no patience for.

"You feel warm. Peta get a glass of water." She picked up a bottle of tablets and gave him two. "These should help."

Niail popped them into his mouth and took a sip from the glass Peta held out to him. "I do not know your name."

"You were too wounded last night to exchange names. I'm Kimi."

Niail nodded. A pain shot through his skull. "I am Niail."

"He's a Hunter." Wil's voice held a touch of awe.

"You mentioned that last night." Kimi pursed her lips. "You also said that you weren't hunting anything. I thought it was just confusion because of the concussion."

"He helps people." Peta sat on the edge of the bed.

"He's a superhero." Wil joined his sister on the bed. "He ran into a lot of bad medicine last night, otherwise he would have beaten the evil guys."

Kimi pulled Wil into her arms and hugged him before guiding him toward the door. "You two scoot. Breakfast is on the table. You had better eat before you're late for school."

When the kids left the room, Kimi turned back to him. Her eyes were clouded with reproach. "I know you probably thought you were being nice, but I would appreciate it if you didn't encourage them."

"What did I do wrong?"

"Life is cruel enough. It's better if they know the truth rather than have their dreams and fantasy shattered later."

"I do not lie."

Kimi tilted her head. "You told them you were a superhero."

"Wil said that. I told them I was a Hunter."

Kimi rolled her eyes. "I'm not going to get angry because I know that you're not thinking properly."

"I know who I am."

"You're a hunter who doesn't hunt animals."

Niail nodded. "We only hunt animals if we need food. Hunters are a warrior race."

Kimi sighed. "There's no point in arguing with you."

"It is not necessary for you to believe. I speak the truth."

Kimi straightened his bedding. "The kids and I need to get to school. You should take it easy until we get back."

Niail could not argue with the advice. His head and body ached. With a grunt of resignation, he slid back down on the bed. What he needed was uninterrupted sleep. Then his memory of the mission would come back, and he could leave.

"Your headache should improve after more rest." Kimi left the room, shutting the door behind her.

The sooner he left the better.

He was too aware of the woman.

It was uncomfortable and disturbing. The last thing he desired was a distraction. His duty was to finish his mission. Just as soon as he remembered what it was, he would do so.

He shut his eyes and concentrated on making contact with one of the brotherhood. Despite the splitting pain that shot through his head, he sent out a mind connection and waited. Usually communication was instantaneous, but not today. His head ached from the effort. No matter how hard he tried, or who he tried to connect with, the result was the same.

Silence.

He was a Hunter alone.

Chapter 2

The classroom door opened and Kimi looked up from the paper she had been marking. Sam, her ex-husband, stood in the doorway. Not now, she groaned inwardly. She had spent the morning arguing with her brother Jake about Sam, and now, here he was. At least he had enough sense not to go to her house.

"What do you want?" Kimi wrote a B in red ink on the paper and put it on her pile.

"I've brought those legal documents for you to sign."

"You don't waste any time." Kimi grabbed another paper. "You just spoke to me yesterday."

"Well, the sooner this is done, the better."

"For you," Kimi whispered under her breath before straightening her shoulders. "I know I agreed to sign them, it's just been a heck of a day."

"Look if this is a bad time, I'll come back tomorrow."

"Tomorrow is Saturday. You would have to come to the house. That would be worse." Kimi threw her pen on her desk. "Jake heard about your visit. I spent an hour this morning arguing with him."

Sam looked up and down the hall before entering the classroom. He shut the door behind him.

"Does he know why I visited?"

"He knows you didn't see the kids." Kimi heard the sarcasm in her voice. As much as she tried not to be affected by Sam's indifference to their children, it infuriated her. He was their father and he would rather brush their marriage and children under the rug. He wanted to pretend it never happened. No matter how much she convinced herself it was for the best, she couldn't understand it. What kind of man walked away from his children?

She had married the man.

What did that say about her?

Kimi blew the hair away from her eyes. "Are you sure you want to do this?"

"It's what Moira wants."

"You never did what I asked when we were married."

Kimi couldn't resist the dig. The truth was that Sam was seldom around when they were married. He was off exploring the world and building his career as a journalist. She had provided a comfortable landing point when he returned.

Sam pulled on the collar of his shirt. "I know I wasn't a great husband. I don't want to make the same mistake."

Kimi stood. "We were kids in college when we married. Someone should have stopped us."

Sam grinned. "Where was your brother then?"

"It's too bad he was in the Forces." Kimi leaned against her desk. "He would have tried to interfere, but I don't think we would have listened."

"No." Sam pulled a folder out from under his arm. "We were crazy in love back then."

"Crazy is the word." Kimi smiled. "That's until reality stepped in."

"I want my new marriage to work." Sam put the folder on the desk. "I know this seems like the coward's way out, but right now I just can't afford child support. I still have student loans. Moira and the new baby are more than I can handle."

"You haven't paid support for years."

Kimi opened the file. A number of legal papers were inside with highlights where her signature was needed. She rifled through them. Words like disintegration, dissolution, and desertion, jumped out at her. Her stomach twisted at the finality of it.

Sam held his hands up in a conciliatory gesture. "I'm the first to admit I've not been a good father."

"What makes you think you'll do better with your new son?"

"Moira won't have it any other way." Sam cleared his throat. "You let me slide at being a husband and a father. You never complained."

Kimi crossed her arms. "I can't believe you just said that."

"What?" Sam frowned.

"You just blamed me for our marriage falling apart."

"It's true. You were too self-reliant. You had to control everything about the kids, and somehow I didn't measure up. I wasn't Blackfeet."

"When we married you were all enthused about living the traditional life of my people."

"That's before I understood what it would entail." Sam waved his arms around the room. "I can't bury myself in this place. There's nothing here for a journalist."

These were the same arguments she had heard throughout her marriage. Sam was still handsome, with his dark hair and eyes, but that's all she saw now. There was no feeling left for him. He was a weak man, who would always take the easy way out. She shuddered to think what life would have been like if the marriage hadn't ended.

She grabbed a pen and started signing the papers. She flipped through all of them twice to make certain she hadn't missed a spot. This was the last time she wanted to see Sam. He was out of her life forever.

She pushed the folder toward him. "You're free. What do you want me to tell the kids when they ask?"

"I'm still their father." Sam picked up the folder. "I care."

"You've been absent for most of their lives. Those are not the actions of a loving father." Kimi sat down and grabbed a paper to mark.

"That's not fair." Sam tucked the folder under his arm. "You know I love them, but you're the one who wants them raised in your traditions. I would only interfere."

"A visit now and then isn't going to corrupt them." Kimi shook her head. "You haven't seen them since Wil was a baby."

"This isn't ideal, but I am trying my best." Sam walked to the door. "They're too young to understand our situation. I think it's best to leave things as they are."

"They're children. All they want to know is that you love them."

"They know that. Thank you for this." Sam motioned to the folder. "It'll be a great help to me."

"Goodbye." Kimi winced as the door shut.

There was nothing left to say.

Sam was out of her life for good.

She looked down at the test papers with unseeing eyes. She had been young and a fool. She had believed that love was all that was needed to make a person happy. She doubted Sam would ever mature enough to make a good father. It was his loss. He was gone. She could close the door on that part of her life now.

Kimi continued to work for another half hour. The bell rang and she packed up the papers and slid them into her drawer. The school day was over. It was Friday and the weekend promised rest.

Then she remembered the man sleeping in her guest room.

Kimi stood and stretched just as a dark-haired woman wearing jeans and a blue blazer walked into the room

"I heard you had a visitor last night."

Kimi grinned at her friend, and fellow teacher, Ann. "News travels fast."

"Is he cute?"

Kimi gathered her books together. "Why don't you come by and see for yourself?"

"That bad huh?"

"He's pretty mixed up." Kimi frowned. "I almost lost him last night."

It had been touch and go at first. Bobby had helped drag him into the bed and then left. The stranger's shirt was torn and the rest of his clothes were in no better shape. She had been too busy wrestling his garments off and tending to his numerous wounds to observe much about him. It wasn't until later that she had noticed the man.

What a man.

He was a giant in comparison to the men she knew. It wasn't just his height, which was at least six feet and a half. He had muscles on muscles. He had jet black hair and when he had opened his eyes, they were dark obsidian. Then there was the matter of his tattoo. He wore a number of symbols that her grandfather claimed were from the Star People.

That might not mean anything, though. Anyone could have found those symbols on the internet, and had them tattooed on them. No, there was something else about the man that was mesmerizing.

He wasn't right in the head of course. His contention that he was a hunter, but didn't hunt animals was just silly. If the tribe had found him poaching they might have roughed him up a bit, or called the police. They certainly wouldn't have beat him to within an inch of his life and left him for dead.

"How did he get to your place?" Ann's voice brought her back to the present.

"Bobby brought him." Kimi shook her head. "The man has tattoos on his arm that look like Star People symbols. My grandfather is out of town, so of course he delivered him to me."

Ann grinned. "You can always trust Bobby to blow something out of proportion. Did you tell Jake about him?"

"Are you crazy?" Kimi's fingers clenched her books. "He would hit the roof if he knew."

Ann opened the classroom door and held it until they were both in the hallway.

"He only wants what's right for you."

"True, but he doesn't trust me to make my own decisions."

They walked outside and Ann stopped beside her blue compact. The clouds hung low in the sky and promised rain. Kimi moved her books to her other arm.

"At least your brother cares." Ann unlocked her door. "I haven't spoken to mine in years."

"I suppose you're right." Kimi glanced at the playground and waved her children over.

Ann threw her books in the back seat of her car and then got in. "Let me know if you need help with the stranger."

"I will."

Kimi waved goodbye and then met her kids at her battered, red truck. It had a king cab and could hold several people. She could have afforded a newer model, but this one moved around the back roads with ease. It suited her needs.

"Let's get home."

She opened the truck door. Peta and Wil jumped in and settled as she put her books on the back seat. The ride home was filled with the children's chatter about their day. The time passed quickly. A flutter of excitement settled in her lower belly when she pulled the truck to a stop in her driveway.

"I hope Niail is still here." Wil unbuckled his seatbelt. "I want him to tell me about Hunters."

Peta jumped down from the truck. "He's a man. He probably left."

Kimi's heart constricted. Peta thought all men were like her father, Sam. He had left without a word of goodbye. Despite her guest's injuries, she should never have let him stay. When he moved on, he would only confirm Peta's beliefs about men.

The house was quiet when they walked in. Everything in the kitchen was how she had left it. Surely he didn't have enough strength to leave? She dumped her books on the table and then opened the guest room door.

He was there.

He was magnificent.

Niail was asleep, sprawled out on the bed with the bedcovers thrown off. He slept on his back, and except for a pair of briefs, he was nude. Her breath stilled as she stared at him. She had never seen such raw beauty in a man before.

Every part of him was massive. Her eyes skittered away from his lower body, but not before she had noted how well-endowed he was. Sam had been average in that department. Size wasn't supposed to matter, but a fleeting curiosity had her wondering if that were true. It took her a second to realize that the kids were pushing behind her.

"Is he here?" Wil's voice was excited. "I need to show him my painting."

Before she could stop him, Wil had squeezed past her, and was at the bedside. He touched Niail's arm and started to shake him awake.

"Let him sleep," Peta ordered from beside her.

Niail jolted and his body tensed. The size and definition of his muscles could have only been accomplished through years of body building. A shock wave went through Kimi, and for a second, she was frozen in place. Whoever this guy was, he healed quickly. His bruises had lightened so that they were almost imperceptible.

Niail's eyes locked with hers and everything faded. She was lost in his dark gaze. She felt her cheeks heat and her breathing slow as the awareness of his strength and masculinity overwhelmed her. She had never been attracted to muscular men before, but she couldn't take her eyes off Niail.

She inhaled a quick breath, and broke the connection.

She needed to keep her distance from this man. He would leave once he was better. She couldn't risk having her heart broken again. The next man she invited into her life would have the same traditions, and heritage as her. He would be Blackfeet.

"Look at the painting I did of you today." Wil shoved his artwork into Niail's face. "The teacher didn't believe me when I said you were a superhero."

Niail pulled his sheets back over his body and then took the painting from Wil. "It shows me with a cape."

"Most superheroes have them." Wil looked about the room. "Mom must have washed yours."

"I am not the kind of superhero who wears one." Niail handed the painting back. "You have talent."

Peta pushed in beside her brother. "Are you staying for supper?"

Niail looked up at Kimi. "You will have to ask your mother."

"You're in no condition to leave for a few days yet." She opened the door wider. "You guys go and start your homework. Our guest needs quiet."

When the kids had left the room, Kimi walked to Niail's bed. "How's your head?"

"It is still foggy." He grimaced. "Every time I try to focus I end up feeling worse."

"Bobby thought you were thrown from a truck." She pulled up a chair and sat down. "Your head hit a rock on the road. He didn't think anyone could survive a blow like that."

"Where did he find me?"

"You were on the southeastern edge of the reservation. He had been out stargazing when he heard the roar of engines. There were gun shots and that's when he ran to see who it was."

"Most would have run in the opposite direction. Bobby must be a brave man." Niail cleared his throat. "Did he see who did this to me?"

She shook her head. "All he saw was the dust of the vehicles, and you lying on the road. He ran after them, but there was no hope of him catching up."

"I am grateful he tried."

"Bobby is my grandfather's apprentice. My grandfather, Eluwilussit, is a healer." Kimi clasped her hands together. "Bobby said a normal man would have died, but other than the near miss we had last night, you seem to be in perfect condition."

"I am far from it." Niail's voice was wry. "My head aches, my brain is muddled, I cannot remember anything about the attack, and I do not know how to contact help."

"Time will heal most of that."

"I hope so." Niail gave her an unwavering stare. "Why did he bring me to you?"

"He saw the markings."

"That is what Peta said." Niail glanced at his arm. "Why should they be important?"

"Bobby thought they made you special." Kimi smiled. "I wouldn't let that go to your head. He thinks everybody is special."

"So you are the person who knows about these symbols?"

"My grandfather is the expert. He's in Billings right now, so Bobby loaded you onto his old pickup and drove you here."

Niail looked straight ahead for a few seconds, and then turned back to her. "I am grateful, but that does not explain why you agreed to take me in."

"I could hardly leave you in Bobby's truck. You would have been dead before sunrise."

"It is not that easy to kill me." Niail's voice was dry. "Many have tried."

"I did notice quite a few scars. I don't know what line of work you're in, but you might think about changing careers."

"There is only one life for a Hunter."

Niail's words were spoken without emotion. There was no eagerness or enthusiasm in his voice, just acceptance. It was almost as if there was no other choice for him. She had never run across that from a hunter before. It was a sport that they enjoyed.

He was awake, and aside from a bad headache, there didn't seem to be any signs of confusion. It was obvious they were talking about two different things.

"What does a Hunter do?"

Niail looked at her without blinking for several seconds. His chin lifted. "We are an ancient warrior race."

For a second, Kimi thought he was joking, but his face and voice were serious. "How old would that be?"

"We have existed since the start of civilization. The Kaladin forefathers altered and modified us to be warriors beyond compare."

Kimi pursed her mouth. It sounded like a fantasy, but who was she to question it? The man believed what he said. Given the number of traditions and stories of her own people, she dare not judge too quickly. He wore the Star People markings. The symbols were considered ancient by the Blackfeet.

"Where did you get the tattoos?"

"They are tokens of my campaigns and achievements."

"Do you know what this symbol means?" She pointed to what looked like two mountain tops with two circles below them."

"Shield."

"Why do you have it?"

"It is the symbol of my clan." Niail rubbed the small tattoo. "I am clan Giath. We are the first to enter a battle. Our aim is perfect."

"My people were given a similar symbol, but it means Protection." Kimi cleared her throat. "Our legends say the Star People came from the heavens and gave us universal laws. The law of protection was one of them."

"So this is why I was brought to you." Niail leaned back against his pillows. "Here I would be accepted."

Kimi nodded. "Bobby was afraid to take you to the hospital. He thought if you were one of the Star People it would be dangerous. The government might take you away."

Niail's dark eyes didn't leave hers. A shiver raced across her head and goose bumps raised on her arms. His eyes spoke of knowledge that she was afraid to know, and yet intuitively, she knew it was necessary.

The truth was in his gaze.

"Bobby is very astute."

Kim looked closer at his arm. There was another symbol she recognized and she pointed to it. It was a circle split in two by a vertical line. "What does this one mean?"

Niail looked at where her finger pointed. "It is a reminder that all Hunters are brothers."

Kimi bit her lip. It was uncanny how similar, yet different, the symbols were. "It means the law of equality for us."

There was one other symbol she thought was familiar. It was the very first marking on his arm and looked like a lower case letter d. It meant the law of creation. "What does this one mean?"

"It was the day I was brought into the world."

Kimi inhaled. "The day you were born?"

"We are birthed outside of women."

A chill went through her.

He spoke as if he were a machine.

She had seen his blood and injuries. He was a man.

"That's a strange way of putting it."

"Since time began, Hunters have been altered and bred to be the best warriors. We do not have parents. We are created."

Kimi looked back at his arm and pointed at the symbols after the sign. "Is this the date?"

"Yes."

"How old are you?"

"I have seen twenty-eight years."

"How long have you been a warrior?

"I was born a Hunter." Niail's voice was low. "I have seen battle for over fifteen years."

Kimi swallowed. "By battle I'm assuming you mean war?"

"There are many battles that do not involve war."

Kimi shook her head. "Who are you?"

"I am a Hunter." Niail shifted on the bed. "One who must rely on your hospitality."

"You're welcome to stay here until you're better." Kimi stood up. "That gash on your head is going to need a dressing change."

"It is not the outside of my head that concerns me." Niail turned to give her access to the wound.

"It should." Kimi unraveled the gauze. "Infections are not easy to fight."

She frowned. Last night it had been an ugly wound that slashed across the right side of his head for several inches behind his ear. There had been gravel and dirt embedded, and it had taken a while to clean it. She had thought it needed stitches. Bobby had insisted she not notify anyone, so against her better judgement, she had just applied antibiotic lotion and gauze.

"Is there a problem?" Niail grunted as he tried to look back at her.

"It's amazing." Kimi muttered to herself. Louder, she added, "It's a lot smaller than last night. I think I can keep the bandage off."

"Good." Niail turned to her. "There is no need to be concerned. We heal quicker in this place."

"By place, do you mean Montana?"

"I mean Earth."

Kimi stared for a second, and then backed away from the bed. He couldn't be saying what she thought. There was no way he was from the stars. The Star People had given messages of peace and harmony. They had not talked of war or battles. Besides, he was human. He might be larger than most, but he was all man. That knock on the head had done more damage than he knew.

"I think I should leave you to rest." Kimi moved to the door. "I have to make supper. You must be starved."

"I would ask that you leave my pants.

Kimi nodded. "They should be dry. I'll put them by the bed."

She closed the door behind her, and for a second she leaned against it. The man had to be confused; there was no other reasonable explanation. If only her grandfather were home. He would know what to do.

She went outside and pulled the pants from the clothesline. The rain had held off all day. There was still a brisk breeze blowing from the north. The rest of the clothes on the line were dry so she took them down also. She folded them into a basket and then brought them inside.

She took Niail's jeans into him and laid them across the bed. He had an arm flung across his forehead and was sleeping. He looked like any other man who had had a rough night. Her eyes shied away from the sight of his fading bruises, though. He did not heal as other men.

With a sigh, she pushed away and set about fixing dinner. The kids were at the table. Peta was doing homework and Wil was coloring. She gave him a quick hug as she went to the fridge and started pulling food out. She had to do something to take her mind off the stranger in her bedroom.

She was draining the pasta when her back door slammed open. She jerked the strainer in her hand, splashing a small amount of boiling water on her wrist. She dropped the colander in the sink and turned to see who the intruder was.

It was her brother, Jake.

"I thought you had said everything you needed to this morning." Kimi lifted the pasta back into the pot and then pumped some cold water on her wrist. It had a quick soothing effect on the burn.

"That's before I heard the utterly stupid thing you did last night."

Kimi's heart beat faster.

She'd been hoping Jake wouldn't hear about Bobby dropping the stranger off at her place. Her brother was overprotective ever since he had joined the FBI. She pulled her hand out of the water, and turned to face him.

"I've done nothing wrong."

"Like hell." Jake's voice rose to an ear-piercing shout. "I thought it was bad enough you let Sam bamboozle you into signing away his responsibilities, but to risk your life and the lives of the kids is crazy."

She crossed her arms. "He was injured."

"We have hospitals for that."

"Bobby thought he would be safer here." Kimi lifted her chin. "I happen to agree with him."

"What is wrong with your head? He's probably a killer for all we know." Jake moved in front of her. "You are making stupid decisions. You'll be lucky if the authorities don't take the kids away from you."

She gasped. "You're my brother. How dare you threaten me?"

"Don't yell at Mom." Peta's voice joined the fray. "He's not a bad man."

"Peta stay out of this, honey." Kimi motioned for her daughter to sit back down. "Your uncle Jake doesn't mean what he's saying. He's just upset right now."

"The hell I am." Jake's voice shook the room. "The guy is leaving now, and I'm going to see to it."

Jake started toward the bedroom door and Kimi ran to stop him. She grabbed his arm. "No."

Jake shook her hand off. "Don't think you can stop me. He goes, and then I'll deal with you."

Before Jake took another step the bedroom door opened. Niail stood there, pants on and chest bare. There was a cold decision in his eyes. Had her brother been right about the man being a threat? Her heart started to pound at a frantic pace. She reached out to stop the inevitable confrontation. Niail was injured, and Jake was a former Navy Seal. Jake would rip Niail's head off.

Then Niail moved.

One step and he reached Jake.

He grabbed her brother by the neck and backed him up against the wall. He held him off the ground. Jake went for his pistol, but Niail was quicker. He had disarmed him in a second, and shoved the gun into the back of his waistband.

"You disrespected a woman and children. You have broken the Sacred Code and deserve to die."

Chapter 3

Jake's words had condemned him.

No man should speak to women or children in the manner, or voice, that this one had. Niail had followed the Sacred Code his whole life. This woman had taken him in and kept him alive. She deserved better than the shouting and disrespect this one had given her.

"You have no honor." His voice was cold with disdain. "You were here this morning, but I was too weak to stop you."

"Let me go." Jake struggled. His fingers tried to loosen the grip around his neck, but Niail held firm.

"Niail." Kimi's voice was a soft plea in his ear. "Let him down. He's my brother and I don't want to see him hurt."

"He disrespected you." Niail didn't loosen his grip. "This morning when he left you were crying. No man treats a woman like that."

"Look, I'm sorry." Jake's voice had calmed. "I'm only trying to protect my sister."

"By threats?" Niail raised an eyebrow.

"I didn't mean them."

"Peta believed you." Niail glanced at the little girl who was sitting at the table, her eyes wide. "Your words do harm."

"You're right." Jake's voice was conciliatory. "Let me down and we'll discuss this."

"Please." Kimi touched his arm. A shock of electricity shot through him. He sucked in a deep breath and felt the ache of his injured ribs. He almost dropped Jake, but he tightened his hold.

"Is that your wish?" He looked at Kimi.

"Yes." Kimi nodded. "He won't do any harm."

"As you command."

Niail released him.

Jake pushed him away and made a swing at his head. Niail blocked it with his arm. Jake swung the other arm and he stopped that too. He shook off Niail's hands. His opponent wasn't finished. Almost on cue, Jake bent his head, rushed him, and hugged him tight about his waist. He tried to force Niail back against the wall.

Pain seared through Niail's bruised ribs, but he suppressed it. There would be time to worry about his injuries after he had defeated his opponent. Niail brought both arms down on Jake's shoulders with just enough force to release his grip, but not enough to break his collarbone. Jake gasped and bent in pain as Niail's knee connected with his chin.

He fell to his knees. Niail hauled him up by his shirt and locked his arm around his neck. Then he leaned close to his ear.

"Next time I will kill you." His whisper was a promise. "Now sit."

He loosened his arm from around Jake's neck and led him to a kitchen chair. He pushed him down and held him there with a hand on his shoulder. Jake sagged against the back of the seat. Niail released him. He grimaced as a spasm of pain shot through his head. He grabbed a chair and sat. The legs shook, but it held his weight.

Wil ran to Niail's side. "Are you okay?"

"You're asking him?" Jake didn't hide his resentment. "I'm your uncle."

"You were mean to Mom." Wil leaned against him. "Niail's a superhero."

Peta nodded. "He's a Hunter."

"I can't believe you did that." Kimi ran a shaky hand through her hair. "Jake's ex-Navy Seal and you're injured."

"He is poorly trained." Niail crossed his arms and winced at the pain. He fought down the nausea.

"No." Jake's eyes were wide. "You're just better than anyone I've ever been up against."

"Niail is a warrior who protects people." Peta started putting her homework into her backpack. "He's from the Star People."

Niail held his breath and waited for Jake's reaction. Their experiences with the authorities on this planet had not been pleasant. All Hunters avoided them. It was safer.

Jake lifted an eyebrow in his direction and then laughed. "I'm afraid he's been telling you some tall tales, sweetheart."

Peta shook her head. "He didn't tell me. He wears the symbols on his arm."

Jake smirked. "Tattoos don't mean anything."

Kimi cleared her throat. "Perhaps not, but until Grandfather returns, he stays safe at my house."

Niail met Kimi's gaze and felt the strong pull of attraction. She was a beautiful woman and she was defending him. It was a unique feeling to have a woman think about him. The life of a normal man had been denied him with the use of implants and enhancers. Since their escape and crash landing on earth, all that had changed.

Niail forced himself to look at Jake. The man was solidly built with the same dark hair and brown eyes as Kimi. That was as far as the resemblance went. Kimi's eyes showed understanding and compassion. There was a coldness and wariness in Jake's expression and stance. His moves showed that he had some military training, but Jake was no match for him.

"You can't still believe that old man makes sense?" Jake's voice held disdain.

"Grandfather is a medicine man." Wil spoke now. "He knows all about the ancient ways and the Star People."

"Those are legends told around the campfire to scare children into behaving."

Kimi inhaled a loud breath. "You have no reason to disrespect Grandfather."

"Those ancient stories have no place in today's world." Jake pushed back his chair. "They'll hold you back. The sooner Wil knows the truth, the better."

Kimi touched her brother's arm. "I know you're ashamed of your heritage, but that's no reason to belittle it."

Jake stood. "Perhaps not, but I've seen more of the world than you."

"More violence you mean." Kimi shook her head. "The Navy changed you."

"I grew up." Jake walked to the door and stabbed a finger at Niail "I want you out of here by Monday, or I start asking questions. I'm sure you won't be happy with the answers I get."

Niail didn't need a human to tell him to leave. He had already stayed longer than was smart. Even if he couldn't communicate with the others, he had to get to a safe place. He might not complete his mission, but he did remember the city his team had last been in.

"I'm sorry Jake was rude." Kimi's voice broke into his thoughts. "He was never fond of the old traditions, but he wasn't so hostile before."

"He carries much anger."

Kimi nodded. "I'm sure you're right. I just don't understand what the people have done to make him that way."

"He has not yet found his place." Niail grimaced as he tried to stand. "He doesn't feel as if he belongs."

Kimi pushed him back in the chair. "Stay seated. I'll get your dinner."

"A woman does not wait on a man."

"You're my guest." Kimi cleared the rest of the papers off the table. "Besides, you're still weak. Tackling Jake must have used up most of your strength."

"I could not let him disrespect you any longer."

"What is the sacred code?" Peta sat up on her knees and leaned her elbows on the table.

"They are the rules that I live by." Niail shifted in his chair. "Your uncle has broken the first law by disrespecting your mother and you."

"Is this code written down?" Wil's eyes widened. "Can I see it?"

"It is written on the Wall of Memories where I come from." Niail pushed back the memory of the last time he had visited the Wall. It had been the day before the Holman, the rebel rulers of Cygnus, had taken his unit captive.

"It makes you sad." Peta spoke with conviction. "Don't you like the rules?"

"A Hunter does not question what he is told. He follows orders."

Kimi put a plate and utensils in front of him. "That doesn't sound very pleasant. Surely you must have some freedom?"

"I did not know what that meant until I came here."

Wil frowned. "You mean the reservation is freer than your home?"

Niail smiled. The simplicity of Wil's mind was new to him. A Hunter never associated with children, even when protecting them. The Kaladin, the former rulers of his home planet Cygnus, had feared that conversing with a warrior might damage or scare children.

Niail leaned back in his chair. "You have choices and that makes a person free."

"You sound like our teacher." Peta took her hands off the table. "He's always saying we should be thankful for the freedom we have in this country. I don't think that's true."

"Why?" Kimi put a large bowl of pasta on the table.

"We're not the same as other Americans." Peta handed her mother her plate. "We once owned all this land, but we're treated differently now."

"Where did you hear that?"

"Daddy used to tell me that all the time." Peta stretched her hand out for her food. "I think that's why he left. He didn't think we were good enough."

Kimi inhaled sharply. "That's not true. Your daddy didn't want to stay with me. He loves you kids."

"Then why doesn't he visit us?"

"He doesn't have the time. He works very hard and is always traveling."

"He was here yesterday." Peta thrust out her lower lip. "He only wants to be with his new family."

"He is a fool." Niail held his plate out to Kimi. "He is less a man for not behaving with honor."

"What does honor have to do with this?" Kimi frowned.

"No man of principle would desert his responsibilities. He would never leave his woman and children." Niail shook his head. "You people do things differently, but some laws are universal."

"Is that part of your sacred code?" Wil's voice was solemn.

"Yes." Niail looked at the boy. "A man of honor does his duty always."

Kimi laughed. "Is there no room for spontaneity in that code?"

"No." Niail knew that wasn't the answer she wanted, but he didn't evade the truth. "We always follow the code."

"What about being happy?" Kimi sat at the table. "Everyone needs joy in their lives."

"We do not care about such things." Niail took a mouthful of pasta. It warmed his hollow stomach. "We have been bred to follow orders and the Code."

"That sounds dreary."

"There is no time for sadness. A Hunter's reward is death."

Kimi hesitated as she put pasta on her plate. "What about family?"

"We do not have such things."

Peta frowned. "You don't have children."

"No." Niail leaned back. "It might distract us from our duty."

"Then your duty sounds stupid." Kimi pulled the salad toward her. "People are more than following orders."

"It makes me glad that you have that freedom." Niail took another mouthful of food. "We make certain that is possible."

"So you sacrifice your own lives so that others can be free?" Kimi's voice shook.

"That sounds like a superhero to me." Peta's voice held a note of awe.

"We have no super powers." Niail rubbed his head. "As you see, I can be injured. It took two people to help me stay alive. I will be forever grateful."

"There is no need to thank us." Kimi relaxed in her chair and started to eat.

Niail continued to fork the pasta into his mouth, but his eyes never left her face. Just looking at her gave him a joy he had never known before. She took his breath away. He would keep her safe and happy no matter what it took.

The meal continued in companionable silence. Niail ate everything that was put in front of him. A warrior never knew when his next meal would be, so he didn't waste. The last few months on earth had meant a steady flow of food, but old habits were hard to forget. He had spent too many years on the front lines to believe that his life was different. He was always on guard.

Niail stood to help clear the table. The room started to spin and he grabbed onto the table. He would have fallen if Kimi hadn't grabbed his shoulder and guided him back into the chair.

"You're still weak." Kimi rubbed his shoulder. "Give it a second and then I'll help put you back to bed."

Wil came to his side. "You should have rested after fighting with Uncle Jake."

Niail grimaced. "You are right." He gripped the table and took a deep breath before forcing himself to stand. He exhaled and pushed back the pain.

"Have a care." Kimi put his arm around her shoulder. "I won't be able to lift you if you fall."

Peta came over to his other side and grabbed his waist. "It's very uncomfortable on the floor."

The three of them made their way to the bedroom. Once Niail felt the side of the bed, he relaxed his weight against it and fell onto its soft surface.

"There." Kimi pulled the covers over him. "I'll let you get your pants off on your own."

Niail heaved a sigh. "That blow to my head has left me weaker than I thought."

"Do you still have a headache?" Kimi walked to the night table and reached for a medicine bottle. "It might be best if you took a couple of these."

Niail held out his hand. He would take anything if it meant the room would stop spinning and the cotton wool in his head would disperse. He didn't know how long this was going to last, but as long as it did, he wouldn't be able to contact the other Hunters.

Kimi and Peta left, but Wil stayed behind. He sat on the chair next to Niail, his eyes wide with concern. Niail was too weary to do more than smile and then close his eyes. Sleep was the only thing that did not take any effort. There would be time to leave when he woke up.

The soft patter of rain against the roof soothed his head. He was weary with exhaustion and pain. Sleep was a welcome relief. A shuffling noise and the whisper of a door closing were the only things that disturbed him before he fell into utter oblivion.

The first thing he noticed when he awoke was that it was daylight. The second thing was the silence. Nothing stirred either inside or out. He glanced at the chair beside the bed. It was empty. Wil had probably spent the night in his own bed.

He focused his mind connection and reached out to Partlan, his team leader. A shimmer of blue and red lights danced near his eyes and then a searing pain knifed through his head. He clenched his jaw and forced himself to push through the agony, but it was useless.

There was no answer.

He was alone.

Somehow he must find his way back to his fellow Hunters. Reaching them was his only chance of survival. Niail threw back his covers and sat up. He needed an alternative way to contact his brothers.

Chapter 4

Kimi looked up from the lesson plans she had been preparing for her classes. Niail stood in the doorway, shirtless. His short black hair was ruffled and there was two days' worth of stubble on his chin. His abdomen muscles tensed as he raised a hand to his head.

"Where are the facilities?"

Kimi grinned and pointed to the open door on the left. "It rained last night so there's no problem with water supply."

Niail nodded. "Thanks."

Kimi pushed away from the table. "A quick shower might help you feel better."

"I don't want to impose."

"The sun is shining so there's plenty of hot water." Kimi opened a closet and started pulling things out. "Here are some clean towels, a razor, and a fresh shirt."

Niail frowned. It looked like he was going to say something and then stopped. He followed her directions and the door closed. Kimi went back to her work and tried to concentrate, but the image of her guest kept intruding.

He was gorgeous.

She'd seen great looking men before. None of them had affected her like Niail. There was almost an invisible connection with him. She sensed him all the time. That was crazy, though. He was an ordinary man.

Extraordinary was a better description of Niail. She shivered when she remembered how he had manhandled Jake the previous night. Her brother never lost a fight. Even before he had joined the Navy Seals, he had been unbeatable. He had finally met his match with Niail, though.

The sound of the shower filtered through to the

kitchen. Kimi glanced back at the lesson plan and sighed. Now that he was awake she wouldn't be able to concentrate on school. She gathered the papers together and threw them in her briefcase. Niail would be hungry when he had finished showering.

She had whipped up pancake batter by the time Niail came out of the bathroom. His face was clean of stubble and he looked years younger. The shirt she had given him was small and stretched over his chest. Every muscle was defined when he lifted the damp towel toward her.

"Where can I put this?"

"You can hang it on the line outside, or leave it in the utility room at the side door."

"I'll take it outside." Niail turned to the door and then stopped. "Where are my boots?"

"They're in the utility room." Kimi pulled a frying pan off the pot rack over the stove. "Are you hungry?"

"Very."

She smiled and turned back to the stove. She lit the propane burner and within minutes she had a stack of pancakes on the table. Syrup and some fresh fruit completed the meal. She was pouring hot water onto ground coffee when he came back into the house.

"Sit." Kimi put the coffee carafe on the table. "You can eat first and then I'll call the kids in."

"Where are they?"

"They're building a small fort at the top of the hill behind the house." Kimi sat and pushed the pancakes at Niail. "After a fresh rain they like to make certain it's still standing."

Niail filled his plate and started to eat. Kimi poured him coffee and then took a couple of pancakes for herself. They ate for several minutes in silence. It wasn't until Niail had pushed his plate away and was sipping his coffee that he looked up at her.

"I need to contact my team. Do you have a computer I could borrow?"

"We're off the grid here."

Niail frowned. "What does that mean?"

"I have no electricity, telephone, or internet." Kimi put some milk in her coffee. "I'm trying to raise my children as close to a traditional life as possible."

"What tradition is that?"

"I'm Blackfeet." When Niail still looked at her with a blank stare she sighed and put her coffee down. "Native American?"

"I do not understand these terms."

"You don't know what a Native American is?"

Niail shook his head. "No. I have not been here long."

"The Blackfeet existed long before the Europeans settled in North American. We lived here when the Buffalo were plentiful and roamed the plains."

A surge of pride filled Kimi. Her heritage was important. Unlike Jake, she had immersed herself in the ways of her people, keeping the language and traditions alive for those who had forgotten. It was why she lived without most of the modern world's trappings.

"This has been a long time?"

"Since Na'pi, Old Man, created the world. Old Man gave the Blackfeet this land and the buffalo." Kimi lowered her voice. "Many have forgotten the old ways, but I won't let that happen to my children."

Niail nodded. "It is important to remember. Your people must have been here when the Ancients visited."

"Who are the Ancients?"

"They have been on Cygnus since the beginning of time." Niail cleared his throat. "They travel the universe, sometimes helping, sometimes taking what they need. I believe they are what you refer to as Star People."

Was Niail saying what she thought? Did he come from the stars, or was he making fun of her traditions? Her eyes narrowed as she continued to gaze at him. His expression was open and there was no sign that he was lying.

"Are you one of the Star People?"

"No." Niail glanced down at the table before looking back at her. "I am not an Ancient."

"Are you from earth?"

"No."

Her mind swirled with the implications. If he wasn't from Earth, then he was an alien. A shiver went through her. The stories her people told of being visited by people from other planets were true. Those visits were long ago, though. Why was Niail here now? Did this mean the Ancients planned to harm Earth?

"Perhaps if you gave me some information about your life and how you came to be here, I would be less confused."

Niail leaned back in his chair. "I was bred and trained as a warrior."

"By bred, I assume you mean when you were created." Kimi leaned her elbows on the table.

"Yes." Niail's voice was devoid of emotion. "We have been genetically modified since the beginning of time. We are not born of women. We are bred in a laboratory and then taught to fight."

"You had no childhood?" Kimi's stomach tightened. "You weren't raised by a family?"

"We had each other."

"That's inhumane."

"That is how it has been for eons. We begin our lessons as soon as we can walk."

"How was that possible?" Kimi put her hands around

her coffee mug. "You would have been too young to do much."

"We had enhancers and implants to help us." Niail's jaw tightened. "I have been altered to be the best warrior possible. I am clan Giath, which means my genes were improved to perfect my precision and reaction time. I have perfect aim."

"So you're a marksman?" Kimi's voice held a note of doubt. "I didn't think a skill could be genetically coded."

"Many things are possible on Cygnus. It is more advanced than Earth."

"Are other things programed into you?"

Niail nodded. "We were also bred to obey. We were the elite warriors for the Kaladin, who ruled Cygnus since time began."

Kimi took a sip of coffee. There was something in Niail's eyes that flickered when he mentioned the Kaladin. Some hidden hurt or memory that was unpleasant.

"What happened?"

"You perceive too much." Niail frowned.

"I can see it in your eyes." Kimi's voice was dry. "There is something that you are hiding."

"There was a civil war on Cygnus and the Holman defeated the Kaladin. They destroyed or imprisoned all Kaladin except the High Council, and then they ordered the execution of all Hunters."

"But you're alive." Kimi put down her mug and leaned closer to Niail.

"Our leader, Ardal, disobeyed the execution order." Niail's voice held pride. "He chose to let us die fighting so we would have honor in our death."

"You didn't die, though."

"No." Niail grinned. "The Holman ship was filled with inferior soldiers. We defeated them and took over the vessel. Unfortunately it crashed on earth."

"So how long have you been here?"

"It has been almost a year." Niail raised an eyebrow. "We have adapted well to our new home. We also found that there were other Hunters on this planet. They have been here for over thirty years."

Kimi frowned. "They must be old men."

"This planet has advantages for us." Niail shrugged. "We heal faster, we move quicker, we age slower, and with our implants deactivated we can be as normal men."

Normal men? Kimi took another sip of coffee. Niail's eyes had not left hers and somehow she knew his meaning was important. She put her cup down.

"How were you different before?"

"We were not allowed to mate."

"Never?"

"It was forbidden." Niail rubbed a small scar on his right forearm. "Our implants made certain we would not have the desire."

"But surely that has changed since you've landed on earth." Kimi tried to keep the surprise from her voice. "You must have been with women?"

"Only our leader, Ardal, has found his mate."

Kimi's mind drew a blank. She couldn't conceive of a man of Niail's age, and obvious masculinity, never having slept with a woman before.

"If your implants are out, then you can feel attraction for women." Kimi's words were hesitant. "You must have found some that you wanted to mate with."

"No." A flicker of emotion burned deep within Niail's gaze. "The genetic modifications that were done to make us better warriors also intensified our bonding. We desire only one mate."

"What does that mean?"

"We bond to one woman. There will be no others. Hunters will go to any lengths to protect them, including disobeying orders."

"So when you have a mate you become unreliable soldiers?" Kimi shook her head. "That makes no sense. Plenty of men and women fight for their countries and still have families."

"They are not Hunters." Niail's voice was low. "A Hunter forms a pair bond with the woman who is destined to be his one and only mate. They connect not only physically, but mentally, and spiritually. They become one with each other."

"That sounds pretty intense." Kimi forced her voice to remain steady. "I'm not sure that's any different than what humans feel when they're in love."

"A Hunter always knows what his pair bond feels and needs, even if they are not mated."

Silence followed Niail's words. The air crackled with tension and Kimi shifted in her seat. The breath caught in her throat and she had to force herself to look away from the truth in Niail's eyes.

"Why are you telling me this?" Her voice stumbled over the words.

"I am certain you are my pair bond. Until I found you I had no desire to be with another woman."

"That's not possible." Kimi shook her head. "We just met. You're confused because I helped you. Patients transfer their affection to their caregivers all the time."

Niail continued to stare at her for a few seconds and then looked away. "As you say."

Kimi exhaled the breath she had been holding. "Now you're trying to humor me."

Niail pushed back from the table. "I know that in over ten months of having my implants deactivated, no woman has interested me. You are the first."

Kimi gave a crooked smile. "That's a wonderful compliment, but I'm not looking for a partner or a mate."

"This is not something we can choose." Niail picked up the empty plates from the table and brought them to the sink. "If my head was not so foggy, there would be no doubt about whether I am bonding with you."

She went to the stove and lit the burner. She still had pancake batter to cook, and kids to feed. She was attracted to Niail, but she wasn't prepared to be his chosen mate. She was an independent woman raising children. She had worked hard. She wasn't throwing it all away because a man appealed to her.

Niail cleared his throat. "I need to contact my fellow Hunters. Do you have any means of communicating with the outside world?"

"My one and only concession to modern technology is a cell phone. I have children." Kimi smiled. "That means I have to be ready for any kind of emergency."

"It works in this area?"

"There are cell towers everywhere." Kimi flipped a couple of pancakes onto a plate. "The phone is in my truck. Ask Wil to get it on his way into breakfast."

Niail went outside and called for the kids. The children were completely taken with Niail and she heard them answer him immediately. They would be disappointed when he left.

Niail returned to the kitchen and leaned against the counter. "Wil's getting the phone."

Peta walked in at that moment. "Who are you going to call?"

"I must report to my brothers. They will be worried."

"Are they warriors too?"

"Don't be so nosy." Kimi chided. "Take this to the

table."

Peta grabbed the plate of pancakes and banged it on the table before pulling out a chair. She sat with her arms crossed. "I just want to know if they are like Niail."

"Yes." Niail's voice was even. "They are my brothers. I have fought many battles with them."

Peta's eyes widened. "Will they come and help you?"

"It is possible."

"Cool." Peta grinned. "Then we can meet them."

Niail opened his mouth to speak, but was stopped by a shout from Wil. He was out the door before Kimi could turn around. She pushed the frying pan off the burner and followed Niail.

Chapter 5

The boy was bent over a large puddle beside the vehicle. Niail picked him up and held him in a protective hug as his eyes scanned the horizon. There were sparse groupings of ponderosa pine and aspen as far as he could see and mountains in the distance. The roadway was clear. There was no sign of movement anywhere.

"What happened?" Kimi's words came out in gasps as she struggled to catch her breath.

"I dropped the phone." Wil pointed down at the puddle.

Niail eased his hold on Wil. "There was no danger?"

Wil shook his head. "Just to the phone."

Niail put him down. "It is good you are safe."

"You scared me half to death." Kimi's voice held a note of reproach. "I thought someone had hurt you."

"Sorry Mom." Wil bent and picked the phone out of the puddle. "I don't think you can use this."

Kimi took the dripping instrument from Wil. She flipped the back open and pulled out a battery. "I'll try putting it in rice. I might be able to dry it out."

Niail's chest tightened. He had hoped to contact Partlan, but that was not to be. He eased his breathing and started to the house. No point dwelling on something he could not change. He would have to devise another plan for contacting the others. The alternative was not worth considering.

Never had he been left without backup before. Always his brothers were with him, whether it was in battle or in his thoughts. Even when technology failed, there was the mind connection. The injury to his head had changed that.

Niail was truly alone.

Peta was at the door waiting for them. "Is Wil okay?"

"He dropped the phone." Niail picked her up in his arms and moved with her to the kitchen. "He was upset."

"Boy, I bet Mom is too." Peta looked over Niail's shoulder. "You sure can run fast."

Niail grunted and put Peta back in her chair. "I have trained since I was younger than you."

Kimi and Wil followed them into the kitchen. "We'll try and dry the cellphone out. If that doesn't work, then I'll drive you into Browning. You can probably find a way to contact your friends there."

Niail's tension eased. It would only be a matter of hours before he was connected again. Kimi's house was isolated. He would be safe here until they could go to town. He might be on his own, but he was well trained. If a situation developed he would take care of it then.

"You kids need to eat." Kimi put the pancakes in front of the children.

Wil grinned and Peta's eyes sparkled. "Our favourite," they sang out in unison.

Niail leaned against the counter and observed the children. A surge of warmth spread through him. This must be how it felt to be part of a family. Unlike the Kaladin and Holman, humans were still connected with their children. The love between Kimi and the children was tangible and comforting.

When the pancakes were done, Wil and Peta took their plates to the counter. Kimi filled a kettle with water from a hand pump at the sink and put it on stove to heat. She started to clear the table, but Niail stopped her.

"I can put this away. You need to sit."

He gathered the syrup and butter and put it in the fridge and then cleared the rest of the dishes. He stacked them in the sink and when the kettle had heated he started washing.

"I understand you want to keep your traditions, but why do you live without running water and electricity?" Niail looked over his shoulder. "Would it not be quicker to have some conveniences?"

"Mom doesn't want us to have the internet or video games." Peta rested her chin on the table. "She thinks it will corrupt us."

"That's not true." Kimi's voice was indignant. "You get the computer at school, and I know you play games when you visit your friends."

Niail frowned. "Why would these games hurt them?"

He had learned his techniques through hand to hand demonstrations and multi-media interactions. All his military strategies and manoeuvers had been burned into his memory during video sessions when he was barely Wil's age.

"I don't want them focusing on violence. The Blackfeet believe all living creatures are sacred."

"So these games go against your traditions." Niail took a seat at the table. "Are all games violent?"

"No." Peta shook her head. "My friend and I bowl on her game console."

"You play with dishes?"

Wil giggled. "It's a game with a ball and pins."

"Your language is confusing."

"Not for me." Wil pushed back from the table. "Peta and I are going back to our fort. Niail, come and help us. We could use someone who is strong to lift stuff."

"I will join you later."

Niail watched the two children run out of the house with a sense of wonder. They were carefree and happy. He had never been either of these things. He would like to spend time with them, but he knew his first priority was getting in touch with Partlan.

"How did you learn English?" Kimi's voice made him turn back to her. "Is it very different from your language?"

"We do not have words that have two meanings." Niail grinned. "It makes things easier to understand."

"So you didn't know English when you crashed?"

"No. At that time we were connected with our translating devices. The language was sent directly to our brain. Now of course, we would not be able to do that."

"That's because you removed your implants." Kimi nodded. "So they were more than tracking devices."

"They were also enhancers." Niail leaned back in his chair. "Most things have more than one use. What is good for one may be bad for another."

"Not being tracked is more important." Kimi sighed. "Living without the conveniences of the rest of the world means I have total privacy. Except for my cellphone, there is no way for us to be found through electronic devices. Someone has to physically locate us."

"You worry about people knowing where you are?" Niail frowned. "Is this a problem in your country?"

"Not for me." Kimi leaned toward Niail. "Jake thinks I'm crazy, but he's not the best person to listen to. He's always in trouble."

"He does not accept easily."

"That's an understatement." Kimi laughed. "Right now he's on suspension from the Bureau. He's supposed to stay away from investigations, but I bet he's following someone that will get him in trouble again."

"He has a strong sense of what is just."

"Yes." Kimi sighed. "I just wish he could see that it's okay to be Blackfeet."

"He must find his own path."

Niail touched Kimi's hand that rested on the table. A jolt of pleasure traveled up his arm and lodged in his lower gut. This woman affected him. He saw an answering response in her eyes. She was aware of him also.

With his brain muddled, he could only rely on his body's reactions. Ardal had told them that as his bonding grew stronger with his mate, he had known her thoughts and feelings. Niail couldn't mind connect, but he knew what he felt.

Desire coursed through his veins.

She was as aware of him, as he was of her. Her fingers fluttered under his hand and his body hardened. Never had that happened before. He inhaled and relished the sensation.

He wanted more.

Hesitation and fear lurked in Kimi's eyes. She wasn't ready to surrender to their bonding. She needed time. Niail straightened his shoulders. He would prove her wrong. Deep in his bones he knew that she was his pair bond. With or without the mind connection, he would be linked to her always.

No matter what she wanted from life, he would be there for her. He would never interfere in her choices or plans. He would protect and care for her. One day, she would see that they were bonded as one, and hopefully, she would chose him as her mate.

Before that could happen, Kimi had to learn to trust him. The best way to do that was to support her.

"The children asked for help." Niail released her hand. "Where can I find them?"

Kimi stood. "I'll take you up there. I want to look at my water pressure tank and cistern. All that rain last night, means everything should be full."

"You do not get your water from the kitchen?"

Kimi grabbed a light jacket and waited for Niail to leave the house before shutting the door. "The kitchen's pump is attached to the well. That's mainly for drinking water. I use rainwater to supplement our washing."

"This system sounds complicated."

"I'm used to it." Kimi pointed to the home that was built of logs. "My family and friends helped build the house and set up the alternative energy system, but I've had to learn how to maintain it."

"This is how your people used to live?"

Kimi shook her head. "Not even close. This just allows me to control the things that enter our house from the modern world. In the summer, when school is closed, the children and I move into a tipi and try our best to live off the land."

Niail frowned. "That is an unusual thing to do."

"I know." Kimi sighed. "I want them to know the best of both worlds. There are some traditions I could never accept, but it is important to remember where we came from."

"I can understand." Niail looked around at the forested landscape, and the mountains with their snow-caps in the distance. He took a deep breath of the fresh pine scent. Humans were fortunate that their planet was still alive.

"We had nothing like this on Cygnus. The water and atmosphere had been destroyed eons ago. Everyone lived within giant pods that had artificial atmosphere and scenery."

"How horrible." Kimi shuddered. "It would be claustrophobic. I need space."

"People do what they must to survive."

"True." Kimi rubbed her arms. "Heritage is more than where you come from. It's also the customs and language."

"I am a Hunter. We do not know where we come from, only that we exist to serve and obey. We are warriors and protectors."

"That's sad." Kimi stopped. They were several feet higher than the house and a large tank was perched beside them. "You have no sense of your heritage."

"My fellow Hunters and the Sacred Code are all I know."

"I understand why it's so important for you to contact them." Kimi's hand rested on his arm. "This afternoon I'll drive you into Browning. My computer is at the school. You can use it to contact them."

Gratitude filled Niail. "Thank you."

"No problem." Kimi turned and examined the tank. "Everything looks fine here. Let's go and play with the kids."

Play?

It sounded intriguing.

He had never done it before.

The rest of the morning was spent building a fort. It started out as an outline and when they were finished they had taken fallen logs and branches and made walls. It was one room with an entranceway. Wil and Peta were pleased.

After lunch Kimi tried the battery in her cellphone, but it wouldn't work. Niail watched as she bit her lip and then heaved a sigh. She grabbed her purse from the sideboard and headed to the door.

"Come on kids. We're going into town."

Niail followed them out of the house. Kimi was already behind the wheel by the time he sat in her truck. She turned the key and nothing happened. She tried it a second time and still nothing. The engine was not starting.

"The battery's dead." She hit her hand against the steering wheel. "Did you notice anything when you got the phone Wil?"

"The door was open a bit." Wil was in the rear seat. Kimi exhaled. "The door light drained the battery." Niail sensed her frustration. "How far to Browning?"

"It's several miles away." Kimi looked over at him. "You can't walk there."

"I am used to walking distances." Niail opened the truck door.

"Not after the injuries you sustained."

"I have had worse."

Niail stepped out of the truck and started down the drive. He had to reach the other Hunters before they gave him up for dead. He might never be able to mind connect again. It was imperative that he find them.

"Wait." Kimi ran up behind him. "You don't have to walk. Someone usually stops by to check on me during the weekend."

Niail hesitated. He could see that Kimi was worried. He had been trained to obey women. Since crashing on earth, they had learned that women on this planet often made decisions based on emotions. This wasn't logical. Uncertainty about whether Kimi was ordering him to stay or making a suggestion made him question her further.

"I can reach the town. Just tell me which direction."

"It's too dangerous." Kimi clasped his arm. "You're injured. Bobby was insistent you stay hidden here."

"That was when I was unconscious." He turned toward Kimi and put his hands on her shoulders. "I will not be captured again."

"It's getting late. The sun will be down soon. I would feel better if you stayed."

Niail's eyes roamed over Kimi's face. Her brow was creased and she was biting her lips. She was sincere in her concern. His response was immediate. His body jolted with purpose. The last thing he wanted was to upset her. He would honor her wishes.

"Then I will remain here until tomorrow."

Kimi smiled. "Great. We could even try to use one of the batteries I have for the solar system."

"No." Niail started back to the house. "Tomorrow is soon enough for me to leave."

His fellow Hunters might not understand, but there was nothing he wouldn't do to keep Kimi happy. Her desires were the only thing that he cared about. His pair bonding was growing stronger. He would contact the others when he could. Until then, he would stay.

The rest of the day was spent outside. The kids played and Niail stayed near Kimi. She worked on the gardens. She weeded the flowerbeds while Niail turned the earth in the vegetable patch at the rear of the house.

"Is this how your people would have lived traditionally?" Niail wiped the sweat from his forehead with the back of his hand.

Kimi laughed. "They followed the buffalo. They didn't stay in one place long enough to grow food."

"So why are you doing it?"

Kimi shrugged. "With this much space, it would be silly not to live off the land a bit. I don't have any animals, but in the summer, it isn't a problem to tend the garden."

"I would have preferred to move around like your ancestors."

"You have itchy feet like my ex-husband." Kimi shrugged. "I always wanted a stable home. My parents died when I was young and my grandfather raised Jake and me."

"So that means living in one place?" Niail frowned. "I can understand, but if you are bonded to each other, does it matter if one of you moves around?"

Kimi stood. "I don't think Sam and I considered how long we would be together. We were young and foolish."

"You and Sam are no longer mates." Niail didn't miss the flicker of pain in Kimi's eyes.

Kimi took off her gardening gloves. "Sam has a new wife and son now."

"And this is why Jake was upset the first morning?"

Kimi turned back to the house. "Jake is angry at everything."

Niail followed her into the house. The longer he spent with Kimi the more he was able to sense her feelings. The subject of Sam had upset her. Trying to understand without being able to connect fully was a challenge. One he had never had to deal with before.

In the past, he followed commands. He took the position he was told to. He killed when he was ordered to. He obeyed. He never contemplated strategy. It was automatic; part of his training. He had relied on his commander to decipher their enemies' motives and emotions.

"I do not want to distress you with my questions." Niail stood behind Kimi as she washed her hands in the sink. "I am trying to understand why you deny what you feel."

Kimi shook the water from her hands and reached for a towel. When she had finished she turned to face Niail. She was within a few inches of him and his stomach tightened. The scent of her filled his nostrils and it took all his strength not to pull her into his arms.

"This attraction between us is crazy." Kimi's gaze seemed to penetrate to his soul. "You're not right for me. I need a man who understands my goals and people."

"My bond grows stronger each minute I spend with you." Niail's fingers caressed her face. "My injury is preventing you from understanding the depth of our connection."

Kimi shook her head. "It has no future."

"I will honor whatever you decide." Niail's kept his voice steady, even though it felt as if he were breaking in two.

Kimi's eyes widened and he was lost. Surely she would not deny him one kiss. He leaned close and waited. She didn't disappoint. Her hands clasped around his neck and she pulled him in close.

Niail wrapped his arms around her waist.

He brushed his lips across hers and felt his heart thundering in his chest. The world spun as his tongue slid across the crease of her mouth. She sighed and opened for him. All thought vanished as he was swept into a maelstrom of sensations and feelings.

His body hardened.

He pulled her closer, feeling the frantic beat of her heart against his own. Reality disappeared and in its place was paradise. How could he ever let her go? He was bonded to her. His very existence depended on keeping her near.

Kimi twisted her head away and ended the kiss. Her eyes were glazed with passion as she struggled for breath.

"That can never happen again."

Chapter 6

Kimi bit her lip and turned back to the stove. Niail was helping Wil with his coloring and Peta was supervising. Peta was sitting on her knees and leaning against Niail. She was trying to teach him the finer points of using crayons.

"You have to stay in the lines." Peta pointed at Niail's picture. "Didn't you ever color before?"

"No." Niail leaned closer to the book. "Our training was the only thing we had time for."

"You must have taken a break?"

"We changed from one educator to another. There was too much to learn. We couldn't waste the precious time we had. Knowledge could mean the difference between living and dying."

"It's not easy being a superhero." Peta's voice was low. "You don't have to worry. I can teach you coloring."

"All kids learn to color." Wil's voice was encouraging. "You will learn fast."

Niail grunted. "I do not seem to be coordinated."

"It's okay to be messy at the start." Peta picked up a yellow crayon. "Try this color on the moon."

Kimi closed her eyes for a brief second. How could her children be so accepting of Niail? They had only known him since yesterday, yet they believed in him totally. They wanted to be near him. She wanted the same thing, but she couldn't risk getting hurt. There was a strong attraction between them. That didn't mean it was meant to be. She had learned her lesson with Sam, and she wasn't going to mistake sexual attraction for love everlasting.

That kiss they had shared had been amazing. Never had she experienced anything like it; certainly not with Sam. There had been a total connection between her and Niail.

They had become one and for a few seconds, she had allowed herself to be lost in the sensation. Then fear had taken over.

He was a stranger.

Worse, he was an alien.

She shouldn't have let her children near him, but there was no stopping it now. They adored and worshiped Niail. Not just because they thought he was a superhero, but because they liked him. Watching them together, she knew the feeling was mutual. Niail would do anything for her children.

So why was she hesitant to accept him into their lives? Niail swore there was a bond between them. One he said that was permanent and lasting. He'd also said he liked to move around. Her life was here on the reservation. That meant any kind of relationship between them would be long distance. She had tried that with Sam and it had been a disaster.

Niail wasn't Sam though.

Dare she trust him?

With a shake of her head, she banged her spoon on the side of the pot. Thinking like this was getting her nowhere. Niail was leaving tomorrow. The only reason he had stayed today was because she had begged. Once he left, he would realize that there was no bond.

"Supper's ready." Kimi left the stove and started to pull some plates from the cupboard. "Clean the table off."

For the rest of the evening Kimi couldn't take her eyes or mind off Niail. He was larger than life and his presence filled her small house. When it was time to put the children to bed, Wil insisted that Niail tell him a story. Peta climbed up on Wil's bed as eager as Wil to hear the story.

"What kind of story do you want to hear?" Niail's voice was uncertain.

"How did you become a superhero?" Wil snuggled deeper into his covers.

"I am a Hunter. I can only tell you about that."

"How did you come to earth?" Peta pulled a blanket around her shoulders. "Did you come on a spaceship?"

Niail glanced over at Kimi. She was standing in the doorway and nodded. She wanted to hear how he ended up here also. As far as she knew there were no regular visits from aliens, at least none that the government admitted to.

Niail cleared his throat. "We were sent to this planet to be executed."

Wil inhaled sharply. "They wanted to kill you?"

"We were no longer needed."

"Why didn't they just let you quit being a Hunter?" Peta was frowning. "You could have gotten a different job."

"We were bred to be warriors. There is no other job for us."

"Why don't you tell us about your home planet?" Kimi thought that was a better place to begin than death. "I don't want you two having nightmares tonight."

"Your mother is right. I come from a planet called Cygnus. There are many classes of people there, but those who rule are the Ancients."

"They've been there the longest?" Peta nodded. "Are they good or bad?"

"They rule." Niail pulled a chair close to the bed and sat. "Long ago when the universe was new, they existed. They traveled the stars and found many other planets and when they saw other creatures that showed potential, they asked them to join them. That is how Hunters began."

"You came from a different planet first?" Wil leaned closer to Niail. "Do you know where?"

Niail shook his head. "It was so long ago that our origins have been clouded by time."

Kimi found herself fascinated by Niail's story. She moved into the room and sat on a small desk chair. She put her elbows on her knees and rested her chin on her hands. Niail looked at her and smiled. A surge of joy raced up her spine.

"I was raised on Beligia. It is a moon of a large planet close to Cygnus, where the Kaladin ruled. It is very similar to earth, but we only stayed until our training was finished."

"Where did you go then?" Peta's eyes were wide with curiosity.

"I was stationed on Cygnus at one of the Kaladin palaces. That was when I was assigned to Ardal's unit."

"Who is Ardal?" Peta asked.

"He is clan Rioge. They are leaders, skilled in all areas of combat and strategy. Ardal is the greatest of leaders because he chose to let us fight rather than die. That is how we came to be on earth."

"If you have a spaceship, why did you stay on earth?" Wil frowned.

"We crashed on your planet." Niail's voice was heavy with sadness. "Many of our unit did not survive. We have no way back, so we have made earth our home now."

Wil yawned. "Do you have a job?

"We help people who seek justice." Niail stood. "That is enough for one night."

"Will you tell us another story?" Peta gathered the blanket around her shoulders and jumped off the bed.

Niail looked at Kimi with a raised eyebrow.

"We will have to wait and see," Kimi answered. "Now it's time for bed."

She shuffled Peta to her bedroom. Niail waited for her in the kitchen while she saw that both the children were tucked into bed. He was frowning and she sat in the chair beside him.

"Do you miss Cygnus?"

"No." Niail shook his head. "Perhaps it was our destiny to find your planet. We have found that there are great injustices here and that many people require our services."

Kimi wasn't sure she wanted to hear about the type of work that Niail did, but she had to ask. "When you said that you righted wrongs, how do you go about doing that?"

"People contact us for help." Niail cleared his throat. "When honor has been forgotten and the truth distorted, there is often only one solution."

"Death?" Kimi's voice was a whisper. "How can violence be the answer?"

"Evil does not allow any other choice." Niail lowered his voice. "We cannot allow the Sacred Codes to be broken. When women and children are threatened and hurt, it is my duty to defend."

"How can you be sure your codes are right?"

"Some laws are universal."

Kimi bit her lip. She knew that her grandfather considered the symbols and messages of the Star People to be universal. She couldn't deny Niail's logic. The Blackfeet believed that no one was born evil, and that truth and honesty were the basis of an honorable life.

"What if a person repents?"

"You want us to give them a second chance?" Niail's voice held doubt. "It has not been my experience that people change."

"There is always hope."

"That is not realistic." Niail shook his head. "If there is true grief for one's actions, then we will allow them the time to restore their honor."

"So your code allows for forgiveness?"

"When it is warranted." Niail sighed. "Lack of knowledge and understanding are usually the only reasons to grant this."

Kimi smiled. "At least there is the possibility."

"This gives you peace."

She nodded. "I would hate to think you were incapable of mercy."

"I have seen too much violence not to feel compassion." Niail reached out and put his hand over hers. "A Hunter does not have time to reflect on his actions. We are forced to act and then move to our next mission."

"That must have changed since landing on Earth."

"No." Niail squeezed her hand. "We are in constant demand."

Kimi's stomach churned at the sadness in Niail's voice. She knew there were problems in the world. She didn't have to look further than her neighbors to know that people fought and hurt each other every day. To think that the services of a group of alien warriors were necessary was overwhelming.

"Are we that horrible?"

Niail shook his head. "No. I find humans to be one of the most understanding and loyal of all races."

"Then why is it necessary for you to continue killing?"

"There will always be those who are greedy and uncaring of how they fulfill their wishes."

Kimi sighed. Niail was right. There was very little an ordinary person could do about corruption or greed. Most people were just trying to survive. Human nature and limited resources almost guaranteed that some would climb over others to get what they wanted.

"I suppose it was perfect on Cygnus."

Niail leaned back in his chair. "If it had been perfect, there would have been no need of Hunters."

"How was it different?"

"Women rule on Cygnus."

Kimi's eyes widened. "What about men?"

"They serve women." Niail's face was expressionless.

"Seriously?" Kimi didn't bother to hide her shock.

"Women make all the decisions. Men do their bidding. Men still have jobs and careers, but everything is directed by women."

"Do they get married?"

Niail shook his head. "Women change their partners frequently. There are no permanent relationships."

"But they still have children."

"Children are born outside of women. They are reared in schools until they are old enough to take their position in society."

"That's horrible." Kimi didn't hide her disgust. "It sounds so cold and unemotional."

"I do not believe they find it that way." Niail held her gaze. "You can understand why a Hunter's desire to bond would not suit the Kaladin, though."

"You don't think all women are like them?"

"Since I've been on earth, I realize that there are differences." Niail's voice was dry.

"I'm sorry." Kimi gave him a rueful smile. "That was a dumb question. It's just so different."

Niail leaned toward her. His mouth softened into a smile. For a second she wondered if he were going to kiss her again. Her stomach fluttered in anticipation as she felt his breath against her cheek.

She longed to taste him again.

Desire flickered in his eyes.

It was as if he could read her thoughts. Niail's hands cradled her head as his thumbs caressed her cheeks. His gaze never left her face. He leaned closer and brushed his mouth against hers. She closed her eyes and surrendered to the sensations his touch aroused.

His tongue stroked the crease of her lips until she opened for him and then he dove in. Swirls of pleasure skittered across her body as her tongue dueled with his. Passion built and time was lost, as they embraced in a world where only the two of them existed.

His hands moved down her back and pulled her from her chair. He held her on his lap, his fingers feathering across her neck and down her chest. A jolt of need settled in her womb as he cupped her breast, letting his thumb stroke across her nipple. A thrill of exquisite pleasure throbbed through her.

With a sob she pulled away. She was crazy to be doing this. What kind of mother would allow a stranger to make love to her while her children were sleeping nearby? Her chest heaved as she tried to catch her breath.

"I shouldn't have let that happen." She leaned her forehead against his. "I'm not like those women from your planet. I don't sleep around."

"We were not sleeping." Niail's voice was dry.

She shook her head. "I've only ever been with one man, Sam."

"He is no longer with you." Niail brushed her hair from her face. "Do you still desire him?"

Kimi shook her head. "No, but I need to love the man I go to bed with. He needs to love me and my children."

"And you do not want that with me?" Niail sighed.

"I don't know what I feel for you." Kimi put her hand on his chest. She could feel the rapid beat of his heart. He had been as affected by their kiss as her.

"Everything is happening too fast for me."

"Bonding can be like that."

Kimi moved off Niail's lap and stood. Her legs were shaky so she held onto the table. She didn't know if her feelings were real or just a reaction to the nearness of Niail. Until she could sort things out she needed to keep her distance, though.

"I think it's best if we both go to bed. You're still recovering and you need your rest."

Niail looked at her for several seconds before nodding his head. "I will not rush you."

Kimi smiled. "Thank you."

"I could never do anything that would bring you despair." Niail stood. He brushed a finger across her lower lip. "I only want your happiness."

Without another word, he walked to his bedroom and shut the door. Kimi sagged against the table. She didn't understand why he affected her so, but he did. Until she knew, she would have to keep her distance from Niail. The sooner he left to find his fellow Hunters, the better.

Sleep was a long time coming for Kimi. She tossed and turned, going over every conversation she had had with Niail. Finally, exhaustion claimed her. The sound of Wil's voice woke her.

He sounded scared.

It was probably a nightmare. She pulled her clothes on and left her room. The house was in darkness. Just as she entered Wil's bedroom, the flash of headlights shone through her front windows. Who would be driving at such a late hour?

"Another bad dream?" She went to Wil and brushed his hair away from his forehead.

Wil nodded. "I want to sleep with you."

A car door slammed and then there was a knock at her side door.

"Someone's at the door." Kimi pulled the blankets up around Wil's chin. "When they leave, I'll come in for you."

She went to the side door, but turned when she heard movement behind her. Wil was shuffling out of his bedroom and headed for Niail's room. She was about to stop him when the banging on the door got louder.

Chapter 7

He awoke with a start. Kimi was talking to someone in the kitchen. He strained to listen, but he did not recognize the voice. Niail's ears were trained to pick up the slightest of sounds. It was a man, but not Jake. His voice was a low murmur.

He moved to sit up, but stopped when a hand touched his arm. "I don't think it's safe."

Niail turned and saw the outline of Wil in the darkened room.

"Why?"

"Mom has company."

Niail grunted. "Why aren't you in bed?"

"I had a nightmare and woke Mom up. There was a knock at the door so I came in here."

Niail eased his body into a sitting position. He had slept in his jeans, but his shirt was on the end of the bed. He picked it up and shrugged into it.

"It's cold in the chair." Wil moved closer. "Can I get in with you?"

Niail did not know how to answer. He had never had someone ask to share his space. Perhaps it was time he became comfortable with human customs. He moved over and patted the bed.

"Sure."

"Thanks." Wil gathered the covers around his shivering body. "Mom has been talking for quite a while."

"Who is it?"

Wil shrugged. "I was in here. I didn't see them."

"Where is your sister?"

"She sleeps through anything." Wil's voice was scornful.

Niail cursed silently. He should have heard the knock. In all of his years of training and battle, he had never slept so soundly that outside noises hadn't woken him.

He had never let his guard down before. The family might be in serious danger because of his mistake. He eased the covers away and moved to the edge of the bed.

"You stay."

"Do you need help?" Wil's voice sounded small.

Niail stood. "I will make certain your mother is unharmed."

"Can I come with you?"

"No." He held up his hand. "Here you will be safe."

Wil shrugged his shoulders. In the dim light from the clock, Niail could tell he wasn't happy with being left behind. It was for the best, though. If he had to kill someone, he did not want the boy to see it. He was too young to be exposed to violence.

He had been the same age as Wil when he had shot his first weapon. That was different. He was a Hunter. He did not want the same life for Wil if there was a choice.

He moved to the door.

He cracked it open and looked out.

There was a man dressed in faded denims and a dirty tee-shirt sitting at the table. He had dark hair which hung in two braids on either side of his head. His elbows rested on the kitchen table and he was leaning close to Kimi.

Kimi was focused on the stranger's words. They were speaking in whispers, so Niail tried to read their lips. He wasn't as adept with reading English as he was in his own language, but a few words caught his attention.

Billings.

Danger.

Drugs.

Niail opened the door and stepped into the kitchen.

Kimi looked up, her expression full of surprise. The man gave him a huge grin and stood.

"You're out of bed." He held out his hand for Niail to shake. "I'm Bobby. I thought you were a goner for sure when I picked you up last night."

"His healing is amazing." Kimi pulled out a chair for Niail. "It's almost miraculous."

Niail sat with a grunt, and turned to Bobby. "I owe you thanks."

"No problem." Bobby waved aside Niail's words. "I would do it for anyone. You really pissed someone off, though."

"Do you know who?"

"My guess would be drug dealers. Do you have a beef with any gangs?"

Niail tried to focus on the night of his accident. The fog in his head had been clearing, but no images of the night surfaced. Pain shot like a knife through his temple. He winced and then everything was blank. He shook his head.

Bobby tapped the table. "They're a problem in the area. We have a lot of tourism, and of course the casino. Rumour has it that we're also a popular area for drug traffickers."

Niail's eyes narrowed. "What kind of drugs?"

"The bad junk." Bobby leaned back in his chair. "I'm all for a bit of weed every now and then, but the hard stuff, like cocaine and heroin, really messes people up."

"Then why use it?" Niail frowned. They knew it could destroy their lives, yet they still bought it. He doubted he would ever understand humans.

Bobby shrugged. "They get hooked."

"It's illegal and yet they still get it." Kimi shook her head. "Now the dealers are selling to young children."

"It should be stopped."

Niail crossed his arms over his chest. Humans seemed helpless to maintain the law on their planet. On Cygnus these men would not be allowed to live.

Kimi heaved a sigh. "The police try. When one operation is shut down, another one starts up. It's a battle they can't win."

"Do you know who is in control?" Niail kept his voice neutral.

"Miles Kowal." Bobby held Niail's gaze. "He owns furniture stores throughout the state. His head office and main warehouse are in Cut Banks. That's where he opened his first store."

"He's a pretty big name in the state. He's constantly in the papers meeting with one politician or another. Just last week he dined at the Governor's house." Kimi's voice was doubtful. "I can't see him being involved with drugs."

Bobby frowned. "I've always had my doubts about him running an honest operation. Some of the guys that work for him have bad reputations. After last night, I asked around. My information says that the man is crooked."

"Are you certain?" Kimi bit her lower lip. "An accusation like that could destroy an honest man."

"No doubt about it." Bobby leaned forward. "I saw a number of petty dealers outside his store today. Kowal was out there talking to them. It didn't look to be a pleasant conversation."

"That doesn't prove he's trafficking drugs." Kimi reasoned.

Bobby shrugged. "It's not likely that he was discussing furniture with those guys."

"No." Niail's voice was firm. "The man is involved."

Kimi sighed. "There's nothing we can do about it."

"It was only luck that I was able to help you last night." Bobby lowered his voice. "They had thrown you off the truck and were aiming their guns when a commotion further down the road caught their attention. They drove off with their tires spinning and left you."

"You risked much to save me." Niail was grateful to Bobby. Only his fellow Hunters would have endangered themselves to rescue him. "I will not forget. If you ever need help I will be there."

Bobby grinned. "What can I say? My training as a healer kicked in. Once I saw those symbols on your arm, I knew I couldn't take you to the hospital. You might not have been safe there."

"Do you think my grandfather will know what they mean?" Kimi's voice held doubt.

"Your grandfather is a very wise man. There isn't much he doesn't know." Bobby pointed to Niail's left arm. "How did you get those tattoos?"

Niail glanced at the markings. "I get these after every significant event in my life, or battle."

"Battle? Do you mean war?" Bobby sat up straight. "Are you a soldier?"

"I am a Hunter."

Bobby stared at Niail for several seconds. "You don't hunt animals, do you?"

"No."

Kimi's mouth dropped open. "How can you accept that so quickly? I'm still trying to make sense of the whole thing."

"It's part of the ancient lore. We may not have called them Hunters, but they were warriors." Bobby turned back to Kimi. "Didn't you ever listen to your grandfather's stories?"

"He didn't tell me all of them. He is old fashioned about young women and their knowledge of traditional medicine." Kimi's voice took on a defensive tone. "What do you know about them?"

"I know they live among the stars."

Niail tensed. Had he said something when he was unconscious? There was no other way for Bobby to know about Hunters.

"You're not serious?" Kimi's voice was a half laugh. "Grandfather never spoke about Star People who were called Hunters."

"That's because they were from earth originally."

"What?" Kimi looked at Niail and then back to Bobby. "I don't understand."

"The Star People took men from earth when they left."

"You mean they abducted them?"

"Yes." Bobby looked back at Niail. "It was so long ago I doubt there's anyone in your world who remembers."

Niail shook his head. "We only know that we have existed since the beginning of time. We've been bred and altered to be the best warriors possible."

Bobby nodded. "Some of the native legends speak of only the greatest fighters and leaders being asked to join the Star People when they left earth."

Kimi frowned. "How long ago was this?"

Bobby shrugged. "These legends are from the time of creation. There's no certain way to know, but your grandfather probably has better answers than me."

"Then we need to see him." Niail pushed away from the table. "How soon can we get to him?"

Kimi put up a restraining hand. "Wait a second. You can't just leave now. He's miles away and you're still recovering. By the time my grandfather returns home, you'll be well enough to talk to him."

"I do not need rest."

"You're speaking to the woman who nursed you."

Kimi's voice was dry. "Don't forget I helped you back to bed last night. Sit down."

Before Niail could obey, there was the sound of slamming car doors outside. Pounding footsteps followed. Adrenaline started to pump through his body and he braced himself for battle. The door was kicked open, and six men with guns rushed into the room.

Chapter 8

Shock and disbelief paralyzed Kimi. Before she could react, she was grabbed and pushed behind Niail.

He was massive.

Her face was pressed into his back.

When she tried to look around him, his arm held her in place. That's when the first jolt of fear raced up her spine. Who were these men? Worse, why had they barged into her house with guns?

"What do you want?" Bobby's voice shook.

"We've come for him." A deep voice boomed from the doorway. "Hand him over and there'll be no trouble."

Bobby moved away from the table. "What's he done?"

"The boss doesn't like questions." The same man answered in a threatening tone.

Kimi peaked around Niail's back. The man aimed his rifle at Niail's head. The rest of the intruders chuckled. It was a low menacing laughter that chilled Kimi to the bone.

She felt Niail's body tense and then relax. "I will come, but first you need to step outside."

"We're the ones giving the orders."

"There are women and children in the house." Niail's voice was low. "This is not the place for a discussion."

"Is that what you think we're having?" The man snorted. "I'll give you to the count of three to move. Then, I start shooting."

"Your words condemn you." Niail's voice was a growl that sent a shiver of dread through Kimi.

Niail pushed the solid oak table over and shoved her behind it. Bobby jumped down beside her. Niail lunged at the lead man, and shoved him into the others. She watched with horror as Niail grabbed the man's weapon and shoved it to one side.

Niail pushed against the men, backing them up toward her side door. Before they were outside the lead man grimaced and threw his weight into Niail. It was useless. Niail flung the man's weapon hand against the doorjamb. The gun dropped to the floor and Niail clasped his neck with a vice-like grip. Another intruder from behind aimed his gun at Niail, but Niail deflected it up.

Kimi put her hands over her ears and ducked behind the table. A blast from a gun reverberated through the kitchen. There was a second shot, a loud scuffling noise, and what sounded like breaking bones. Loud screams and groans filled the air. Then there was silence.

Fear knotted her stomach.

Footsteps sounded on the floor.

Her body shook as she ducked lower. Next they would come for her and Bobby. She was helpless. She prayed that the children would stay in their rooms.

The table was pushed away.

She was pulled up into strong arms.

She stifled a scream just as Wil opened the bedroom door. She struggled to get loose, but she was held close. It took several seconds before she realized that the arms were trying to soothe her. Her breath caught in her throat. She forced herself to look at her captor.

It was Niail.

He was gazing at her. His eyes dark and emotionless, yet she sensed he was making certain she was unharmed. Her body sagged with relief. Niail and the children were safe.

"I'm fine."

"Good." Niail released her. "Wil go back to bed and shut the door. When it's safe I'll tell you to come out."

"I heard gunshots." Wil's voice sounded small to her ears. "Are you hurt?"

"It takes more than a bullet to stop me."

At that moment Peta's voice came from her bedroom. "Can I come out too?"

"Stay there honey."

Kimi's voice shook, but she was past trying to hide her fear. Six men had come into her house to hurt her and the children. It would take days, maybe a lifetime, before she would be able to forget the horror of it.

Her lower lip trembled and she forced back a sob. She almost jumped as Niail's finger touched her chin and raised her head so that she was looking into his eyes.

"You are safe." His voice was low and sincere. "I will always protect you."

Words failed her. She couldn't answer, so instead she nodded and then sat on the last upright chair. Someday this would make sense. For now, she focused on trying to make her body stop shivering. The after effects of fear were wreaking havoc on her.

Her eyes refused to leave Niail.

The man's gaze was mesmerizing. She was drawn to him and even though she hadn't moved, she sensed his protective embrace. She felt him reaching out to her. It was as if he were silently sending her reassurance.

"Thank you." She took a deep cleansing breath. "I'll be okay."

Niail nodded and then turned to Bobby. "We need to get rid of the bodies before the children come out."

Bobby nodded. He put the table back on its legs and picked up the napkins that had fallen to the floor. It was a mundane activity. Kimi sensed that Bobby was trying to calm his nerves. Niail stood as if nothing had happened. He was calm. He waited until Bobby had settled himself.

"Let's go."

The two men left the house, closing the door behind

them. She glanced around the room looking for anything out of place. There was nothing. Other than the chairs on their side, there was no evidence of the struggle.

Her brain was numb. It refused to believe what had happened here. Her house was isolated. To have men come on the reservation and threaten them was insane.

Time crawled as she waited for the men to return. Her mind shied away from what they were doing. It was better if she didn't think about the killing. Ten minutes later, they walked into the house.

Bobby went to the sink and scrubbed his hands. Kimi saw the slight tremor of his fingers as he held them under the water. She turned to Niail who was waiting at the door.

"Was anyone alive?"

Niail shook his head. He held three hand guns. He went to the antique sideboard that stood at the end of the dining area and pulled open a drawer. He stuffed the weapons in before turning back to her.

"You need protection."

"That's horrible." Kimi's mouth went dry. They would have to contact the authorities and report the deaths and the weapons.

"They meant to kill us." Niail's voice held no emotion. "I had no choice."

"You do this often?"

Niail nodded. "It is the work of a Hunter."

Kimi put her hand up to her mouth and fought back her nausea. How could he stand there and calmly admit that killing was a part of his life? She abhorred violence. She believed as her grandfather had taught her; the sacred force lived in all beings.

"You have lived a sheltered life." Niail moved toward her. "You do not know the life of a Hunter."

"How can I trust you with the children?" Her voice

was a whisper.

"It is forbidden to kill or harm a woman or child." Niail squatted down in front of her and gathered her hands in his. "I have never broken the Sacred Code and I never will."

Kimi's hands trembled in his. At the same time a jolt of awareness shot through her body. She had never had such a reaction from touching a man. She looked into his eyes and her breath caught in her throat. He had felt it too.

"Is that a promise?"

Niail squeezed her hands. His gaze never left her eyes. "I vow that I will die protecting you and the children."

His words and voice held a truth that she had never heard before. Her heart started to beat faster. She didn't care who or where he had come from. No man on earth had ever given her such a promise.

"I believe you. Thank you for protecting us." She bent and kissed the top of his head. There was nothing sexual about it. It sealed his vow.

"Now we must leave."

Niail stood and moved to the door. "Pack a small bag for the children and yourself. Bring some food if you have any, but we cannot stay here any longer."

He motioned to Bobby. "We need to drive their truck off the reservation. It cannot be found here."

"Gottcha." Bobby joined Niail. "You follow in my truck."

Then they were gone.

Kimi was alone in the kitchen.

She took a deep breath and picked up the fallen chairs. When all was in order she went to the hall closet and pulled out a small athletic bag. Focusing on what she needed to pack kept the horror of what had just happened at bay.

"Kids, you need to gather your things." She moved to

Wil's room first. "We're going away for a little while."

She shoved a clean set of clothes and an extra pair of underwear and socks into the bag. She did the same for all of them and then thought about Niail. He had pants, but his top was beyond repair. She looked through her spare closet and found an old coat of Sam's and a sweatshirt. That would keep him warm for a bit.

When she went back to the kitchen both Wil and Peta were sitting at the table. They had their school backpacks in front of them. Their faces were grave and somber. Her heart clenched. They were too young to deal with what had happened here this evening.

"I'm sorry kids." She plopped the bag on the table and gathered the children to her. "I should have listened to Uncle Jake and asked Niail to leave yesterday."

"He was hurt." Peta looked up at her. "He needed help."

"Niail stopped the bad men." Wil sat back in his chair. "Those men would have hurt us."

"He's the reason those men came here." Kimi tried to keep her voice calm, but Wil wasn't wrong. Those men would have hurt them whether Niail was here or not. They would never have believed that they didn't know where he was.

"He's a superhero." Wil hugged his backpack. "Niail will take care of us now."

Kimi sighed. "I hope so. We'll probably go to Uncle Jake's and ask him for help."

"Uncle Jake won't understand." Peta went to the cupboard and pulled out some granola bars. "We need to take some goodies with us."

"You sit down. I'll pack." Kimi shushed her daughter away. "How do you know we need food?"

"We're not deaf Mom." Peta sat with a sigh. "We

heard everything. When the men broke into the house I hid under the bed."

"I watched at the door." Wil's voice dropped to a whisper. "Those men aimed a gun at Niail and he still pushed them out of the house."

"You didn't see anything else I hope?" Kimi couldn't keep the dismay from her voice.

Wil shook his head. "Niail blocked everything and once they were outside it was too dark to see."

"Thank God." Kimi hugged Wil close. "Niail didn't want you children to be involved."

"He protected us." Peta leaned her chin on the table. "I'm glad you helped him Mom."

"So am I." Wil pushed away from Kimi. "He talks different from everyone else. I think he really is one of the Star People."

Just then there was the sound of a vehicle pulling into the driveway. She motioned the children into one of the bedrooms, shut the door and then leaned against the counter. She would know soon enough if it were friend or foe.

Bobby opened the door.

Kimi relaxed. "You can come out kids."

Niail entered.

He had blood on the side of his tee-shirt.

Her eyes widened.

"You're injured."

Chapter 9

Dismay and alarm filled Kimi. Her heart sped up and for a second, fear froze her in place. Why hadn't she seen he had been injured? Niail had rushed a group of men with weapons. She should have checked him. Instead, he had been concerned about how she was doing. She stumbled toward him.

"It is a scratch." He picked up a towel and wiped his side. His eyes searched the room as if looking for danger and then he turned to Kimi. "We left their vehicle at the side of the road."

"How long before it's found?" Kimi took the bloody towel from him and ran it under cold water.

"They'll find it before morning." Bobby put both hands on the back of one of the chairs. "I think you guys should hide up in the mountains."

"Are you crazy?" Kimi shook her head. "It's June. The nights are still too cold."

"Maybe, but where else will you be safe?"

"Will your brother, Jake, help?" Niail touched Wil's shoulder as the boy ran up to him. "I can take you there. Or is there someplace else?"

"What about you?" Kimi picked up the sweatshirt she had pulled from the closet and handed it to Niail. "Your head still isn't right, plus you have all those other injuries."

"I heal fast." Niail picked up another towel and turned away from Kimi before pulling the clean shirt on. "My head injury is no reason to endanger you any further."

Peta put her backpack on. "Should we call Uncle Jake first?"

"We cannot stop to make a call. Time is important." Niail handed Wil his pack. "What about you, Bobby?"

"I'm heading to the bush." Bobby shrugged. "I don't trust anyone now."

"I understand." Kimi grabbed her bag. "Are you taking your vehicle?"

"I'm leaving it on the road." Bobby started out the door. "I've got emergency gear in the back. It's not safe to go near my house."

"That is wise." Niail steered the children out of the house.

"We need a boost." Kimi pulled out her keys. "The battery in my truck is dead."

"No problem. I'll pull up in front of you."

Niail took the lead to Kimi's truck. "How will you know when it is safe for you to return?"

"I'll keep in contact."

Bobby jumped into his vehicle and drove it close to them. He pulled the hood latch and then jumped out with cables in his hands. Within a couple of minutes Kimi's truck was running.

Bobby jumped back into his vehicle and leaned out the window. "Good luck."

"Thank you." Niail opened the truck door for Kimi.

Kimi settled behind the wheel and waited until everyone was in before putting the vehicle in gear. Jake's house was about forty-five minutes away in Cut Bank. When they reached the main road, she turned the radio to a country station. The music had the desired effect. It wasn't long before the kids were asleep in the back.

Kimi cleared her throat. "I think that I should take the kids to my friend Ann's house until we've spoken with Jake. There might be delays once the authorities are involved. At least at Ann's they will get their sleep."

"Will they be safe?"

"No one will look for them there." Kimi spun the

wheel of the truck around and headed toward her friend's house. "Tomorrow is Sunday so I don't have to worry about them missing school."

"I wish I could remember why those men were after me." Niail spoke in a low voice. "I never meant to endanger anyone."

"I know." Kimi reached over and clasped his hand, almost reeling from the surge of electricity that coursed through her. "I wouldn't have turned you away even if I had known what was going to happen. It's not your fault."

"Your brother will not think so."

"Leave Jake to me." Kimi smiled. "He's been different since he came home, but he's still my brother. No one knows him better than me."

"It is comforting to have a brother you can rely on."

Niail looked out the window. The dark night outside made the reflection of his face clear. His features were grim. Kimi knew he was thinking of the other men he had been trying to contact today.

"You will find them." Kimi cleared her throat. "You're not alone. I'm here for you."

Niail turned back to her. "That gives me great pleasure."

Kimi frowned. "I shouldn't have insisted you stay with me. It was selfish."

"It was necessary. Those men would have killed you and the children."

Kimi's breath caught in her throat. "You can't be sure."

"I have dealt with men like that my whole life." Niail's eyes narrowed. "They have no honor. It would have been easier to defeat them if my brothers had been here."

"You handled it fine on your own."

"It was sloppy."

"How many other Hunters are there?"

"We were a full unit when we crashed." Niail's voice was grim. "Not all of us survived."

Kimi bit her lip. What the heck was she to make of that? He had killed six armed men by himself? What would a whole unit of Hunters do? The world couldn't handle that much violence. He had said he would protect her and the children, but what about other people?

"We are not a threat to humans."

Her eyes widened and she turned to look at him. "How did you do that?"

"What?" Niail leaned his head against the headrest.

"It's almost as if you read my thoughts."

"My head hurts too much for that."

"Does that mean you can read our thoughts normally?"

Niail shook his head. "No. Your face is very expressive. I have some training in reading people's expressions and words."

Kimi's grip on the steering wheel lessened. He was observant. She would have to watch out for that in the future. She needed a poker face. She had one small problem, though. She didn't lie and she wasn't going to start now. She glanced over at Niail. His eyes were closed.

She drove to Ann's house in silence.

She pulled up to her friend's small bungalow and shut the engine off. The lights in the house were on and Ann's car was in the driveway. Peta stretched her arms over her head and unclipped her seatbelt. She leaned over the front seat.

"This isn't Uncle Jake's house."

"No. We're at Ann's house." Kimi pulled the keys out and looked over at Niail. "Keep the kids here until I come back."

Niail nodded. "We will wait."

Ann would be curious, but the less she told her the better. The kids needed someplace quiet and safe for the evening. She couldn't trust that Jake would provide that. The door was opened before she even rang the bell. Ann was in her pajamas, with one hand on her hip and a wide grin on her mouth.

"Don't tell me things got too hot with your guest." She squinted at the car. "Is that him?"

"Yes." Kimi cleared her throat. "Could you take the kids for the night?"

Ann's eyes widened. "You need privacy already?"

"It's not like that."

Ann pulled her friend into the house, but left the door open. "Then how is it?"

"It's a bit difficult to explain, but I have to go to Jake's and I don't want the kids' sleep disturbed any more than necessary."

Ann crossed her arms. "Are you in trouble?"

Kimi shrugged. "I won't know until I've spoken with Jake."

Ann bit her lip and glanced out the door before looking back at her. "It sounds serious."

"It is. The less I tell you the safer you'll be." Kimi's voice dropped to a whisper. "I need to be certain the children won't be harmed. Can you watch them for me?"

"Don't worry about anything." Ann hugged Kimi. "How long before everything is straightened out?"

"Tonight for sure." Kim bit her lip. "I don't know about tomorrow. I'm hoping Jake can sort this out quickly."

"I can take them to school on Monday if necessary."

"Would you?" A weight lifted off Kimi's shoulders. "I would feel better knowing they were with you."

"Consider it done." Ann leaned out the door and waved at the truck. "Bring them in."

Kimi went back to the vehicle and opened the door. Niail was already standing outside. "Will you carry Wil in?"

"I must check the house first."

He went to the front door and walked past Ann, disappearing into the darkness, before Kimi could stop him. She shook her head. What could possibly be wrong? Ann was a well-respected teacher, who never got into trouble. But then, so had she been, until tonight. She leaned back against the truck. No point in arguing.

"He just wants to be sure we're safe." Peta's voice was close to her ear.

"I know, honey." She leaned down and kissed her daughter's cheek. "The sooner we get you to bed, the better."

"You're going to Uncle Jake's without us."

"Yes. I hope we can get things straightened out soon."

Niail came out of the front door and walked to the truck. "It is safe."

He gathered Wil in his arms. Peta jumped out beside him and took both backpacks with her. Kimi brought up the rear. Niail waited for Kimi at the front door.

"What have you told your friend about me?"

"I said you were injured."

Niail grimaced. "Perhaps that explains her strange conduct."

"I've known her for years, and nothing explains her behavior."

Ann was waiting for them in the living room. "You can put them in the guest room. It has two twin beds."

Niail followed Ann's direction and went into the room with Wil. Kimi led Peta to the opposite bed.

"You children should sleep now." Niail pointed to the first bed. "Climb in."

Wil tugged on his shirt and reached up. Niail hugged

the boy and watched as he scrambled into the bed.

"Don't let Uncle Jake arrest you."

"I will be careful." Niail pulled the covers over Wil. "It is certain death if a Hunter is caught."

"So you'll leave us?"

"I cannot stay here. You are in danger if I do." Niail perched on the edge of the bed. "I will be close by. I promised to protect you and your mother. I will not go back on my word."

Wil nodded and pulled the blanket under his chin. "That means I'll see you again."

"Yes."

"I'm glad." Peta's sat on the opposite bed. "I like you."

"I like you too." Niail stood. "Go to sleep."

When they entered the living room, Ann was waiting. "I have to talk to Kimi for a second."

"Do you have a phone I could use?" Niail glanced around the room.

Ann picked up a cordless phone and handed it to him. "Be my guest."

When Niail started to dial, she grabbed Kimi and pulled her into the kitchen. "Why didn't you tell me he was such a hunk?"

"He was injured." Kimi shook her head. "That was the last thing I was thinking about."

"Injured or not, that man is nice eye candy."

A cough from the doorway sent heat to Kimi's cheeks. When she looked at Niail, she knew from his expression that he had heard Ann's comments.

"We need to leave."

Kimi nodded. "I'll phone you when I can."

"Don't worry. The kids will be fine with me." Ann led the way to the front door. "You take all the time you need to straighten out this mess."

They went back to the truck in silence. It wasn't until they were on the road to Jake's that Niail spoke. "Your friend has strange ideas."

"She means well." Kimi glanced over at Niail. "I didn't tell her the whole story, so she's bound to come to conclusions on her own."

"Are you certain the children will be safe?"

"Ann will take good care of them." Kimi turned back to the road. "Were you able to contact the other Hunters?"

"No." Niail glanced over at her. "The telephone number I have for them is not in service."

Kimi frowned. "Why would that happen?"

"It is standard practice to disconnect cell phones if they have been compromised."

"You're alive, though."

Niail cleared his throat. "If one of us is captured there is always a remote chance that we will talk under duress."

A shudder went through Kimi. "Are you talking about torture?"

"It has been tried in the past."

"Not on this planet I hope." Kimi took her eyes off the road and looked at Niail. His jaw had tightened and he was looking straight ahead. His silence told her more than she wanted to know.

Kimi's hands tightened on the steering wheel. "If you can't use the phone, there must be another way to contact them."

"I can use the internet."

"We should be at my brother's in another twenty minutes." Kimi stomped on the gas. "After Jake sorts this out we'll use his computer."

When they arrived, she parked the truck in front of the door. They went up the front steps together. She rang the doorbell and waited for Jake. He pulled the door open a couple of seconds later. His eyes widened when he saw who was there and then he unlatched the screen door.

"Come in." His voice was harsh.

Kimi dropped her bag in the living room. "We need to talk."

Jake looked at her for a second and then walked into the kitchen. They followed him. He pulled out a chair and sat.

"You had better tell me fast."

"Don't act like that Jake." Kimi sat opposite him. Niail stood at the counter, his body tense and alert.

"You showing up at this time of night can only mean bad news." Jake raised an eyebrow. "Who is it? Grandfather?"

Kimi shook her head. This was worse than she had expected. Jake's face was hard and unmoving. Niail stood rigid with arms crossed. These two men might be enemies, and yet they were more similar than different.

"There was a problem at my house." Kimi twisted her hands in her lap before looking her brother in the eyes. "We had a visit from some men."

Jake frowned. "Who?"

"Bobby thought they were Miles Kowal's men."

Jake stood and shoved back from the table with such speed that he sent his chair flying to the floor. "How the hell did they come to be at your house?"

"They came for me." Niail moved to stand beside her.

"Why?"

"I have no memory of meeting them, but Bobby thinks they might be the men who left me for dead."

Jake glared at Niail, his eyes bulging. A muscle twitched at the side of his face and for a few seconds Kimi thought he was going to have a stroke. Then, he exhaled and swung around. His fists beat at the air and he shook his head before turning back to them.

"Are you one of Kowal's contacts?"

"I do not associate with criminals." Niail held Jake's gaze. "Kowal is a criminal."

Jake nodded. "We've had him under surveillance for several months. Just when we think we've got a break in the case, someone disappears."

"Did you have him watched two nights ago?" Kimi hoped her brother could give her an answer that would explain why the men had shown up at her house.

"Yes." Jake heaved a sigh. "We lost him for about a half hour and when we had caught up, he was alone. We don't know where the men with him went."

"Was I one of those men?"

"What kind of person do you think I am?" Jake's voice rose in disgust. "I would never have let you stay at my sister's house if I had recognized you."

Niail nodded. "Good. I can trust you then to protect Kimi."

"She's my sister for God's sake. What do you think I would do?"

"You did not act honorably yesterday." Niail's voice held a note of rebuke.

"That's how families are. It doesn't mean we don't love each other." Jake shook his head. "You're clueless about people."

"Niail doesn't have a family like we do." Kimi's voice was low.

"Okay, I'll overlook your lack of tact." Jake picked up his chair and sat down. "Now what happened to the men who came to your house?"

"I took care of them."

"What's that supposed to mean?"

Kimi held her breath. Jake was a hothead, especially when people didn't follow the rules. He wasn't going to be happy with Niail's solution.

"I killed them."

Chapter 10

Niail was fascinated by Jake's reaction. The man had been a soldier. He should have understood the necessity to kill. Instead, he was pounding his fist on the table and hollering. Niail let the noise reverberate in his head for a few seconds before grabbing the man's arm.

"Enough." Niail thrust away Jake's hand. "It was necessary."

"How do you plan to explain that to the authorities?" Jake was spitting his words. "You've told me, and there is no way I can ignore it. It's against the oath I took when I accepted the badge."

"Then you must tell them the truth."

"I have to take you under custody." Jake shook his head. "Do you understand what I am saying?"

"You want to arrest me."

"You're darn right I do."

"It wasn't like that." Kimi stood up. "He was defending us. Those men burst into my house carrying guns and threatening us."

"They had guns?" Jake frowned. "How the hell did you manage to overtake them all?"

"I am proficient in such things." Niail walked toward the kitchen doorway.

"I'm skilled and there's no way I could do that."

"You are not a Hunter."

Jake rolled his eyes. "That's supposed to mean something to me?"

Niail shrugged. There was no point in arguing. Jake did not understand. He was not trained and bred as an elite warrior. He had not killed his first man when he was ten. He had not fought his first battle when he was thirteen.

They were miles apart in experience and knowledge. There was no training that could replace the genetic modifications given to him. Being on Earth gave him even greater advantages with speed and strength, not to mention healing.

Niail walked into the living room. Was his training putting Kimi and the children at danger? It was him that they had come for. If only his memory of the mission would return. Then he could understand better what his enemy wanted.

There was only one solution.

He must leave.

He walked to the window. There was darkness everywhere. He could see the reflected light of the kitchen mirrored in the window. He needed to use Jake's computer to contact his team. Then he had to tell Kimi he was going. His heart lurched at the thought.

Even though he had seen his own leader Ardal claim a mate, he had not believed in the legend of pair bonds. He had never felt any attraction to a woman before. Even with his implants removed and living among humans for almost a year, there had been no desire to mate with one. That had changed the moment he had looked into Kimi's eyes.

When those men had burst into the house his only thought had been to protect her. At that moment, he had understood why he was drawn to her. He could almost read her mind. Kindness and gentleness shone from her eyes. If his head had not been so confused after the hit, he would have been certain sooner. He no longer had doubts.

Kimi was his pair bond.

She was his mate.

Wounded and unable to mind connect with his fellow Hunters, he had been given the gift of a pair bond. It was incomprehensible why a warrior like him would be linked with a mate. His value to his unit was his marksmanship. There was nothing outstanding about him; no reason he should be chosen. He wasn't going to question the workings of the universe, though.

His path was clear.

Kimi must be protected.

He rubbed his side. A bullet had grazed him at the house. It was a constant ache, but minor. He would tend to it when Kimi was safe. He turned away from the window when a flash caught his eye. He stepped back and watched for several seconds. The light was repeated, but this time it was closer to Jake's house. He waited. He counted three separate signals. That could mean only one thing.

They were being stalked.

He moved back to the kitchen. Jake opened his mouth to speak and Niail put his finger up to his lips for silence. Kimi stood and frowned. Worry was evident in her eyes. Niail fought the urge to hold her and wipe the anxiety from her eyes. Now was not the time.

"We are being surrounded."

Jake's eyes widened. "Who would dare?"

"Someone who knew you were working on a case against Kowal." Kimi held her hand up to her mouth. "There's no time. You have to call for backup."

"I can't do that." Jake's voice was serious.

"You are not working within the law." Niail knew the truth before Jake answered. There was only one reason someone would not call for help. They were disobeying direct orders. "What do you want to do?"

"I'll call my partner Mark."

Niail grabbed Kimi's hand. "I am leaving with Kimi."

"You can't just take her." Jake's voice rose. "She's my sister. She stays with me."

"No." Niail pulled Kimi close. "Kimi and the children

are my responsibility. I will not go back on my word."

"Okay." Jake raised his hands. "Wait a second. Let me call Mark and then I'll go with you. We can strategize together."

"I have no need for plans. We have weapons and that is enough."

"You can't shoot your way out of this."

"Why not?" Niail walked to the door with Kimi following him. "I have the guns from the men who broke into the house earlier."

"You can't use those and expect me to turn a blind eye." Jake grabbed his arm. "I'm a FBI agent."

Niail stopped at the front door. "I do whatever it takes to protect."

Jake put his hands on his hips. "Let me call Mark, then I'll come with you."

Niail looked at Kimi. She hadn't said a word since he had taken her from the kitchen. "Do you want to wait?"

"We can't leave him here." Kimi turned her face up to him, her eyes beseeching him to understand. "He's my brother."

"Then we will wait." Niail shifted his gaze to Jake. "Phone him now."

Jake nodded and then turned back to the living room. He picked up his cell phone and made a quick dial. "Mark, we have a problem."

Niail turned his attention to Kimi. She looked frozen with shock. He pulled her close and rubbed his hand up her back. It was an unusual situation for him, but it felt right. The tight rein he kept on his heart and emotions loosened as Kimi eased against him.

Jake hung up and grabbed his coat. "How do you want to go about this?"

"I am putting Kimi in the truck." Niail turned the

door handle. "Then I will take care of the intruders. You stay with your sister."

"And let you have all the fun?" Jake shook his head. "Not on your life buddy."

"My actions may not be legal."

"The only thing that matters is that we get out in one piece." Jake pulled a gun from a chest of drawers by the door. "Mark will meet us on the reservation."

Niail pushed Kimi behind him. The night was cool and dark. He rushed to the truck, and within seconds, she was lying across the front seat.

"Start the vehicle and wait five minutes." Niail put the keys in the ignition. "If we have not returned, leave."

"Where's Mark meeting us?" Kimi turned to look up at her brother.

"He's going to be at the main road into the reservation. Then he'll follow us." Jake took the safety off his pistol. "We're going to Grandfather's sweat lodge."

"That's where I'll go if you don't return."

"Mark will get you to safety if we fail."

"We will not fail." Niail reached for the guns he had stashed under the front seat. "We might take longer than expected."

Jake shook his head. "Where did you get this guy?"

Kimi smiled. "He found us."

"Five minutes, no more." He shut the door and turned to Jake. "There are three men. Do not get in my way."

He crouched and moved to the cover of the bushes that lined the driveway. Jake followed. He did not have to explain the drill to him. The light came again. Niail watched for a second flash and then motioned Jake in that direction.

He would take the first man and then wait for the next signal. Staying close to the ground the two men inched their way toward their quarry. The sounds of the night masked their approach. They were within a few feet of the watchers and able to see the guns that were braced against their shoulders.

The guns were aimed at the truck.

Waiting was not an option.

Niail jumped the first intruder. He broke his neck before he could send off a warning shot. Jake pulled the automatic rifle away from his opponent. The second light signaled. Niail was upon the man before he could shout a warning. He smothered his cry with his hand before choking him to death.

That left the third stalker.

Niail did not wait for Jake.

He pounced on the man and pulled the rifle up against his neck, holding it there until the life had drained from him. Jake reached him, just as he threw the body to the ground.

"You killed them all." Jake's whisper was incredulous. "What if they had been innocent?"

"They were not."

"You don't know that." Jake raked his hands through his hair. "I can't believe I've gone from a peace officer to a killer."

Niail stood. "I did the killing."

"Is this normal for you?"

Niail picked up the assault rifle. "We do the killing."

"So that makes you insensitive to it." Jake sneered.

"No one gets used to death." Niail walked to the truck. "Did you, when you were a soldier?"

Jake shook his head, his shoulders sagging. "No."

"I am not the enemy." Niail reached the vehicle and opened the door. "These were Kowal's men and they meant harm."

Jake climbed into the front seat beside Kimi. Niail

folded himself into the rear and leaned his head back. The adrenaline leaving his body was being replaced with exhaustion. His head continued to throb and he winced at the sharp pain that shot through his temple.

"You overdid it." Kimi's concern showed in her tone.

Niail closed his eyes. "We have taken care of the threat. Now you need to get us to safety."

Kimi put the truck in gear and started to drive. Within seconds, they were on the road and speeding away from Jake's house.

"How am I supposed to explain this to my superiors?" Jake twisted around to face the rear.

"Their guns were pointed at Kimi." Niail straightened his shoulders. "The last one had his finger on the trigger."

"You can't leave dead bodies lying around." Jake crossed his arms and faced forward. "Even if they are criminals, they deserve the benefit of the justice system."

"They gave us no other option." Niail closed his eyes.

"Your head aches." Kimi glanced back at him in the rear view mirror. "Rest. It will take us a while to get to Grandfather's cabin."

Niail tried to speak, but exhaustion had already claimed him. He fell into a deep sleep and it wasn't until his body was nudged that he opened his eyes. Jake was staring down at him, his hands on his shoulders. Niail started up.

"We're here."

He shook the sleep from his head, but the fogginess remained. He grimaced. The vehicle had stopped and the interior lights were on. Kimi was watching him from the front seat, concern written on her face. He needed to alleviate her fears so he nodded and opened the door. There was no way he wanted her to know how the last two encounters had sapped his energy.

Darkness surrounded them. The night sky was full of

stars that twinkled and shone with a brightness that only a remote area would allow. He inhaled the brisk fresh air.

"The cabin is in those aspens." Kimi came up beside him. "My grandfather often comes here alone."

"The truck needs to be hidden."

Jake reached for the keys from Kimi. "You open the cabin and I'll park behind it. The trees should protect it from prying eyes."

"What about your partner?"

"Mark knows the drill. He's waiting." Jake pointed to a figure moving out from the trees. "I'll meet you there." He jumped back into the vehicle and drove off.

Mark walked with them to the cabin. Niail waited for Kimi to retrieve the key from under a rock near the door. The pain in his left side had increased, but he pushed it away. There would be time to focus on it later. Now he had to be certain they were safe.

"You guys wait outside until I get some candles lit." Kimi opened the door.

Jake followed Kimi in. "I'll help."

The flickering flames of candlelight started to show through the windows. Mark went in before Niail. A sharp stab of pain twisted Niail's side. He leaned against the door frame and waited for it to pass. Sweat beaded on his forehead, and he wiped a hand over it before entering the cabin.

"You need to cover the windows." He pulled the first set of curtains. "The light can be seen from the outside."

Kimi rushed to the next window and brought down the blind. "We can put towels over the openings that don't have coverings."

When they had finished blocking the outside Niail looked around the small cabin. It was built of log. It had a central woodstove, with a food preparation area next to it.

There was a table, four chairs, and a couch in front of the fire. Bunk beds were in an adjoining room. There was enough space for at least four people to sleep comfortably.

His head swam and his stomach churned with nausea. He pushed back the sensation and took a step forward. His side screamed in protest. Now was not the time to worry about an injury. He looked at Kimi and noticed her frowning.

"Are you alright?" She took a step close to him.

"Keep clear of him." Mark pushed her away. "He's one of Kowal's men."

"That's not true." Kimi shook off Mark's hand. "Kowal's men are after him."

"I saw him with them yesterday when I was doing surveillance."

The world started to spin and Niail gritted his teeth. He needed to sit down. He reached for a chair, but Jake pushed him back.

"You son of a bitch." He spat at him. "I trusted you."

Niail swayed and then everything went black.

Chapter 11

Kimi screamed as Niail fell to the floor. She rushed to him and pushed him onto his back. That's when she noticed the blood. She pulled his shirt up. He had made a makeshift bandage from one of her kitchen towels. A strip of torn fabric held it in place. It was soaked in blood.

"He said it was only a scratch," she muttered under her breath. She hadn't even seen him take the towel to cover it. "We need a first aid kit."

Mark snorted. "Let him die."

"How dare you?"

Outrage at Mark's callous attitude ripped through her. All life was sacred. Her chest tightened as she realized Niail must have been in great pain since the attack at her house. He had continued to fight despite that.

Kimi went to the cupboard and pulled out drawers until she found the kit. There were a couple of bottles of water on the shelf. She grabbed one to clean the wound. He had risked his life to save her. There was no way she was going to let him die.

"He was left for dead by Kowal's men." Kimi shot Mark a look of disgust. "He is not one of them."

"He probably double crossed Kowal."

"How do you know?" Kimi went back to Niail and knelt beside him. "Kowal's men are after you and Jake. That doesn't make you criminals. Niail needs help."

An eerie hush descended on the room.

Kimi looked up.

Jake was frowning. His hands were on his hips and he was staring at his partner. Mark had his arms crossed and eyes narrowed as he returned Jake's gaze. Suspicion and distrust flowed between the two.

"You told me you were going home." Jake broke the silence.

Mark shrugged. "It was a last minute thing."

"Why should I believe you?"

"I'm your partner for God's sake." Mark shook his head. "You're paranoid."

"True." Jake held up his hands in a conciliatory manner. "This business of Kowal's men showing up at my house has me a bit antsy."

Mark's hand ruffled his hair. "I saw this guy talking to Kowal himself. If he isn't one his men, then he knows something."

"He can't remember." Kimi pulled the towel away from Niail's side. "Someone shot at him and left him for dead on the side of the road."

"Is that why he's hurt now?" Jake walked over to her.

Kimi shook her head. "No. He only had the gash on his head and scrapes and bruises when Bobby brought him to me. This is new."

"Looks like a gunshot."

"It's from the men who came to the house." Kimi bit her lip. "He rushed them even though they had guns."

Her fingers shook as she touched the ragged edges of his wound. The bullet had grazed his side, but it still looked ugly and raw. She didn't want to consider what would happen if Niail didn't make it. She had to focus. She took a deep breath and poured bottled water into the gaping hole in Niail's side.

"He's certifiable." Jake held his hand out for the water. "Give me that. I have emergency first aid training."

Jake used gauze to examine the wound. "The bullet passed along the side of his chest. It barely missed his ribs. It looks worse than it is."

Kimi released the breath she'd been holding. Her whole body trembled at the thought of Niail dying. In just a couple of days he had become important to her. She watched Jake clean the edges of the wound and then pull it together with steri-strips before putting another dressing on it. Niail had lost blood, but he should recover.

"Can we get him up on the couch?"

"He weighs a ton." Jake closed the first aid box. "Put a pillow under his head and get a blanket. He can sleep on the floor."

Kimi brushed the hair from Niail's forehead. "He's still suffering from a concussion."

"A hard surface isn't going to make him worse." Jake stood. "Besides, what if he falls off the couch? It's pretty narrow for a man his size."

He was right. She stood and grabbed a pillow and afghan from the couch. She would stay with Niail. The thought of leaving him was unbearable. She was connected to him.

He wasn't like any other man she had ever known. She abhorred violence, but she didn't blame him for what he'd done. There were few choices once the men had barged into her house.

He had saved her life.

She couldn't abandon him.

She put the pillow under his head and covered him with the blanket. She would wake him in a couple of hours to be certain that the concussion was cleared. Now she had to concentration on their plan to get help. Hiding here wasn't getting them any closer to safety.

"How long before Kowal finds us?"

Jake's voice interrupted her thoughts. She pulled her gaze away from Niail. "Why should he find us?"

"You tell me Mark." Jake stood in front of his partner.

Mark crossed his arms. "I am not working with Kowal. I'm undercover and trying to put him behind bars just like you."

"Why didn't he visit your house?"

Mark shrugged. "I wasn't home when you called. Who knows? He might be there right now."

Jake grunted. "You had better not be lying."

"Look man, we have to trust each other, or we're lost."

"Why can't you call your commander and explain what you were doing? Once he knows that Kowal is after you, he'll understand." Kimi went to the woodstove and started to stack paper and kindling inside. "He'll send someone to help."

"We don't have enough evidence." Jake sighed. "Besides, Mark and I have been doing this undercover stuff on our own. No one sanctioned it."

"So someone might think you both are working with Kowal?"

"Bingo." Jake threw back his head. "I can't believe we let ourselves be hoodwinked like this?"

"I'm telling you, it's this guy." Mark pointed at Niail.

Jake shook his head. "He brought my sister to my place. He's the one who noticed the men outside. If he was working for Kowal he wouldn't do that."

"You said he lost his memory."

"He knows who he is." Kimi struck a match and lit the kindling. "He just can't remember what happened before he was beaten up."

"That's pretty convenient."

Kimi sat back on her knees. "It's common in concussions. From what Bobby said, Niail was thrown off a vehicle at high speed. He hit his head on a large rock, and shots were fired at him. It's a miracle he's alive."

The flames started to lick up to the larger wood pieces. In a few minutes the fire would be blazing and adding heat to the cabin. The only other thing they would need was water, but they would have to go to the creek for that. Kimi wasn't venturing out of this place until daylight. She stood and stretched her hands over her head.

"I don't think we'll solve anything this evening. We need sleep."

"One of us will stand guard." Jake pulled his pistol out of its holster. "I'll take the first shift."

Mark yawned. "I'm not going to argue. I was awake all last night watching Kowal's house."

Kimi went to a small shelf along the wall near the door and pulled out a couple of blankets. She threw one to Mark. "You can sleep in the other room. There are two bunks in there."

When Mark had gone to bed, Kimi gathered a blanket around her and turned to Jake. "Do you trust him?"

"More than I trust that guy." He nodded toward Niail.

"Let's hope you're right."

Kimi walked over to Niail and sat down. She had no intention of leaving him alone tonight. She didn't trust Mark. Jake's intentions toward Niail weren't clear either. Niail deserved to be protected until he could fend for himself.

"You can't sleep there."

Kimi spread the blanket over herself. "Why not?"

"You don't know anything about him." Jake's voice was incredulous. "He's a stranger."

"I know enough." Kimi put her head on the edge of Niail's pillow.

"He could be a psychopath for all we know."

"He's not."

Kimi snuggled into Niail's side. A sense of belonging pulsed through her when she heard him sigh. This was where she wanted to be. She wasn't going to argue with Jake or anyone else about it. The floor was hard, but after a few minutes, the rest of the world faded as sleep claimed her.

She woke to dark eyes staring down at her.

Niail was awake.

"How do you feel?" Kimi covered her yawn with her hand.

"Better." Niail sat up and looked down at his side. "Did you put this on?

"You collapsed." Kimi scooted upright. "The towels were soaked through. There was blood everywhere."

Niail grimaced. "It should have held."

"Why didn't you tell me?" A shiver went through her. "You probably made it worse."

"There was no time."

Niail stood. For a second she thought he might fall again as he grabbed the back of the couch. After a couple of deep breaths, he eased away. She got up and folded the blankets. The fire had died down, and there was no sign of Jake.

She frowned and went to the bedroom. The door was still closed. When she opened it, neither Mark, nor Jake was there. Where had the two of them taken off to? She turned back to Niail, who had pushed aside the curtain on one of the windows and was looking outside.

"It is daylight." He let the curtain fall back into place. "Where is your brother?"

"He said he was taking the first watch. Mark was supposed to be sleeping."

Niail raked his hands through his dark hair. "I have never been felled by an injury before. I failed you."

Kimi went to him and put her hand on his arm. "You should have told me earlier how seriously you had been injured."

"We needed to get away."

Niail clasped her hand and she felt a surge of warmth sing through her body. What was it about this man that made her feel weak, and then strong, at the same time? He looked like a regular man, but he talked, and acted like someone from another place. She had always believed that the Star People were spirits sent to guide humans. Now she knew that they were living, breathing beings, just like humans.

"You lost a lot of blood." Kimi led him to a chair at the table. "You should sit."

Niail shook his head. "I will rest when I know where the others are."

"My brother would never hurt us."

"I trust no one." Niail opened the door. He took the key from its hiding place and put it in his pocket. "I will be the only one who can enter. Lock the door after me."

Kimi watched him walk toward the trees that surrounded the cabin. She bolted the door and then turned back to the room. There was a chill in the air. She banked the ashes of the fire and laid some larger logs on top of kindling. Within minutes, it was a blazing glow of flames. Now all she needed was water.

She pulled the water jug off the counter and put it by the door. When Niail returned, she would get water. She rummaged through the cupboards. There were a few tins of beans and canned meat. She had brought some energy bars in her bag, so she put those on the table. By the time she had finished organizing the supplies Niail had been gone for over half an hour.

Panic clenched at her chest.

Where was he?

At that moment there was a loud retort from outside. She ran to the door, and was about to turn the lock when she remembered Niail's words. She was unarmed so storming out wasn't an option. She glanced at the bedroom door and made her decision.

She ran into the room and crouched down beside the furthest bunk. It was the closest to a window. She heard the rattling of the front door. Niail should be the only one with the key, unless he had been shot. Kimi's heartbeat faltered at the thought. She held her breath when she heard the unmistakeable sound of the door opening.

Someone was inside the cabin.

A second later, the bedroom door opened.

"It is safe."

A surge of relief flooded her. It was Niail.

"That sounded like a gunshot earlier."

"It was."

She stood and went to him. She forced herself to walk even though she wanted to rush into his arms. She needed him near.

"Who was shot?" Her eyes narrowed as she examined him. "Not you?"

"I am unharmed." Niail opened the door wide and waited for her to enter the main room.

Jake was sitting at the table. Beside him was Mark with his hands tied behind his back. Kimi's eyes widened and she looked back at Niail for an explanation. His face was emotionless. He grabbed the water container at the door.

"I will fill this." He opened the door. "It would be best for your brother to explain."

Kimi looked back at her brother. She heard the door close. Her gaze didn't leave Jake. He wiped a hand over his face, before looking up at her. His shoulders sagged, and there was an air of defeat about him. She went to the table.

"I didn't know." Jake leaned back into the chair. "I thought I could trust him."

"How long before they find us?" Kimi kept her voice low.

"He didn't have a chance to call anyone." Jake pulled a cell phone out of his pocket and put it on the table. "There's no reception here. I caught him trying to sneak away in his car."

"Who fired the shot?"

"Mark did." Jake looked down at the table and shook his head. "If Niail hadn't come up from behind, I would be dead."

Kimi turned to Mark. She drew in a slow, steady breath. Now wasn't the time to lose control. They needed their wits about them if they were going to get out of this alive. Who knew what information Mark had passed on to Kowal's men before he had met up with them?

"Why?"

Mark rolled his eyes. "You can't be that stupid."

"I'm assuming you needed money, but why try and kill us?" Kimi crossed her arms over chest, keeping her clenched hands hidden.

Mark shrugged. "We wanted the Hunter. He won't stop coming after us, so we have to be certain he doesn't live."

"You know what he is?" Kimi kept her tone calm. She longed to yell at Mark, but that would get them nowhere. They needed information.

Mark frowned. "It's not exactly a secret. They advertise on the internet."

"There are actually people out there called Hunters?" Jake shook his head. "Why haven't I heard of them before?"

"You're obsessed with catching Kowal." Mark twisted his shoulders. "These guys have rules. All bets are off if you break them."

Jake snorted. "Let me guess, Kowal hired them, but left out the part about him trafficking in drugs."

"Niail said it was dishonorable." Mark spat the words out as if it left a bad taste in his mouth.

"That sounds like him." Kimi smiled. "Was he alone?"

"He's the only one that showed up." Mark heaved a sigh. "It got messy after that."

"How messy?" Jake leaned on the table.

"He injured quite a few of Kowal's men before they overpowered him."

"Then what happened?" Jake's voice had a hard edge to it.

Mark shrugged. "He was taken away. We assumed he was dead, until Kowal went back for the body and it was gone."

"Bobby found him." Kimi shuddered at the thought of what would have happened if he hadn't.

"It didn't take long to figure out where Bobby had taken him." Mark's voice was dry.

"That's why Kowal sent men to my house."

Mark grunted. "Kowal could have handled all of this on his own. There was no need to get outside help."

"Then ask them to leave." Jake rolled his eyes. "If you can find these guys on the internet, surely you can get rid of them?"

"You don't understand." Mark's voice went low. "If you lie they won't stop until you're dead. It's something about honor."

"So now Kowal has a group of mercenaries tracking him." Jake's tone was doubtful.

"Not yet, but if he doesn't kill Niail soon, he will."

"That doesn't explain why you staked out my house." Jake's voice was a growl. "I'm not involved in any of this."

Mark's gaze skittered away from Jake. "Kowal wanted you dead."

"That's why he hired Niail?" A nerve pulsed at the side of Jake's face.

Mark nodded. "He refused to do it."

"Nice to know." Jake's voice was dry. "Does Kowal know where you are?"

"I left a message that I was meeting you." Mark heaved a sigh. "You didn't tell me where we were going."

"And you expect me to believe that?" Jake slammed his hand on the table. "You tried to kill me."

"Anger is not a solution."

Niail spoke from the door. While Jake had been yelling, he had come inside. Kimi's stomach fluttered and her breath caught in her throat. The control he had over his emotions was amazing. If Mark spoke the truth, then he was a mercenary for hire. That didn't fit with what she knew of him. Perhaps the concussion had destroyed more than just his memory.

Niail took the water to the counter and filled a kettle and then set it on the woodstove.

"I told my sister what happened, but there's something I don't understand." Jake crossed his arms over his chest.

"It was simple. Mark aimed a gun at you and I took it away before he could kill you."

"That's not it." Jake's eyes narrowed. "He says you had plans to kill me."

Niail shrugged. "I have already told you what I am. I would not have killed a police officer without a valid reason."

"He says that you are for hire."

"We help people."

"So you answered a request from scum like Kowal?"

Kimi's stomach clenched. Niail didn't deserve Jake's scorn. He had already proven himself. He had saved their lives more than once and he was wounded. He should be in a hospital, not answering Jake's accusations.

"Sit." Kimi pulled out a chair. "Jake can get longwinded."

Niail obeyed with a heavy sigh. "We live by honor. Kowal pretended he was a man with a just cause. We always investigate before we carry out a request."

"That's what you were doing?" Jake threw his hands up in the air. "What if your investigations aren't thorough? That means anybody can ask you to kill someone and you'll do it?"

"I follow orders." Niail's tone was calm. "I can't remember the details of my meeting with Kowal, or even if I did meet him. You only have your partner's word for that."

Jake looked from Mark to Niail.

Kimi knew her brother couldn't decide who was telling the truth. That meant he was going to take both of them into custody. She moved closer to Niail. She wasn't going to allow Jake to arrest him. He didn't deserve to be treated like a criminal. He was the victim.

Before Jake could speak they heard the loud backfire of an engine.

Someone was coming.

Chapter 12

Niail motioned Kimi into the bedroom.

He moved to the door and waited.

Like a thousand times before, he braced himself for battle. He steadied his breathing and slowed his heart rate. There was the sound of stomping feet, then a pause, before the door handle turned. He pulled the door wide as it was opened and blocked the intruder before they could step into the cabin.

An elderly man with grey hair tied into two braids stood there.

He took a step back. The man raised an eyebrow. Niail tilted his head and then motioned the stranger into the cabin before shutting the door.

"Grandfather!" Jake pulled the man close. "I thought you were in Billings."

"I am here now." The old man's eyes roamed the cabin in a slow perusal before coming back to Jake. "Why is your partner tied up?"

The old man turned to Niail. "Who is he?"

Kimi stepped out of the bedroom. "This is Niail, Grandfather. Niail, my Grandfather, Eluwilussit."

Niail nodded at the old man. Steady brown eyes were turned on him; intelligence shone from their depths. Niail's respect for the man grew. The man turned to Kimi.

"Your visit is not for enlightenment."

"No Grandfather." Kimi took the old man's hands. "We are in danger."

Eluwilussit merely nodded and then he went to the boiling kettle on the stove. "I need tea."

Niail led Kimi to a chair at the table. He remained standing at her side. He sensed her anxiety and fear even though it was dissipating since Eluwilussit's arrival.

"So Mark is no longer welcome?" Eluwilussit put the steaming tea he had made on the table. He pulled out a chair opposite Mark. "What have you done son?"

Jake snorted. "What hasn't he done? He tried to kill me. I thought he was working with me to get evidence against Kowal and his men. Instead, I find he's on their payroll."

"Mr. Kowal is a well-respected member of the community." Eluwilussit took a sip of tea. "What is he accused of?"

"You name it." Jake went to the cupboard and pulled out three more mugs. "Drug trafficking, prostitution, extortion, and now hiring assassins."

"Those are strong words. Do you have evidence?"

"You sound like my boss." Jake put a teaspoon of instant coffee in each mug and then filled them with the boiling water. "I have Kowal on video receiving money that came from drug dealers. These dealers are too young to drive. They're kids off the reservation."

"So he sells poison to our children?"

"Yes." Jake put a mug in front of Kimi and then pushed one toward Niail. "Worse, his men have been enticing young girls to work for them. They're babies for Christ's sake, and he has sold them to men double their age."

"Do the girls go willingly?"

Jake shrugged. "It makes no difference; they're not of legal age. The whole business is steeped in corruption and filth."

Eluwilussit nodded. "That is the way of the modern world."

"It's my job to stop it." Jake's voice rose. "They're ruining our children with their drugs and sex trade."

"It is a great sadness. Our youth have lost connection

with their heritage." Eluwilussit glanced at Niail with a raised eyebrow. "Who is this one?"

Kimi straightened in her chair. "Bobby found him. He was injured and I have been helping him."

"He looks as if he can take care of himself."

"I can." Niail crossed his arms over his chest. "These men that Jake speaks of, have been persistent in their efforts to kill your granddaughter. I have vowed to protect her."

Eluwilussit's eyes swept over him in a slow, thorough motion, lingering at the bloody shirt before moving on. "You are still injured."

"He was shot." Kimi reached for Niail's arm. A surge of warmth flowed through him at her protective gesture. "He still has a concussion, but he refuses to rest."

"We rest when the battle is won."

Eluwilussit paused. He lowered the mug of tea to the table and then leaned back in his chair. "You are a warrior?"

"He calls himself a Hunter." Jake snorted.

Eluwilussit nodded. "I have heard mention of them."

"Don't tell me you know what they are?" Jake threw his hands up in the air. "How the hell can everyone else know but me?"

"You do not take time to learn the ways of the people." His grandfather's voice was sad. "You scoff at our legends and teachings."

Jake shook his head. "I've never heard of them in the legends. Wil thinks he's one of the Star People."

"Are you?" Eluwilussit turned his brilliant gaze onto Niail.

"I do not know."

"He wears some of the symbols." Kimi put her hands around her coffee. "Their meanings are close to ours."

"Where did you get these symbols?"

"They are reminders of my battles and events in my

life." Niail pulled up his sleeve. "All warriors wear such things."

Eluwilussit stood and came to look at Niail's arm. He examined it with his eyes and then his fingers traced the symbols tattooed there. Niail sensed a repressed excitement, almost as if the words on his arm spoke to Eluwilussit about something hidden.

When he was finished Eluwilussit pulled the sleeve down and looked into Niail's eyes. He held his gaze for several seconds before turning back to his chair. When he was seated, he pursed his lips and then turned to Kimi.

"You did right to take him into your home. The others would have harmed him."

Jake heaved a sigh. "So is he a Star Person or not?"

"He is one who was taken away. Now he has returned home."

"That makes no sense at all." Jake shook his head and then leaned toward Mark. "What do you know about them?"

"Just what their website says. They right wrongs."

"He's a mercenary." There was no mistaking the loathing in Jake's tone.

Niail moved closer to Kimi. "We protect."

"Is that why you answered Kowal's demands to kill me?"

"I have no memory of what happened with Kowal, but if I had accepted his request you would be dead."

A mere human, whether trained in combat or not, wasn't a match for him. Niail's gaze didn't falter from Jake. Jake continued to hold it for several seconds before lowering his eyes.

He pushed his coffee away. "I'll just have to believe you."

Mark shifted in his chair. "These ropes are uncomfortable. You need to untie me."

"Not until I have answers." Jake leaned back in the chair until it was resting only on its rear legs. "The safest place to speak would be back at the office."

Mark gave him a smirk. "The minute you try and drag me in, Kowal's men will take you out."

"It can't be that easy, or he wouldn't have hired someone else to do it."

"He has enough problems without trying to cover up a killing."

"Now that is interesting." Jake plopped the chair back on its four legs. "What could be keeping his attention occupied?"

Mark turned his head away, but Jake clasped his chin and leaned close. "Tell me."

"Someone else wants his territory."

"Who?"

"The FD Warriors."

Jake released Mark's chin.

Niail recognized the name. They were a feared bike gang heavily invested in criminal activity. The gang controlled most of the illegal ventures in eastern North America and were expanding west. Hunters had been keeping a close eye on their activities.

"We have dealt with them in the past." Niail's voice was cold. "They attacked our leader. They lost. They are not warriors and have no honor."

"You have a leader?" Jake frowned. "That sounds awfully organized."

"We maintain our unit."

"A unit of you guys? That means you're military."

"Yes." Niail raised an eyebrow. Jake's constant doubts were becoming tiresome.

"Great." Jake flung himself back into his seat. "Now there's more than one assassin running around."

"We only kill when necessary."

"You kill for money." Jake crossed his arms. "You're the worse kind of criminal there is."

Niail took a deep breath and pushed back his anger. He required a clear head to plan their next move. Arguing with Jake was getting him nowhere. He needed to resolve this problem with Kowal.

"Your words show your ignorance." Niail motioned to Mark. "A criminal would have let him kill you."

"He's right." Kimi pushed away from the table. "Niail saved your life."

Jake rubbed his hand over his face. "None of this makes sense."

"That does not make it less real." Niail finished his coffee and put the mug on the table. "I am going to check the perimeter."

"I'll go with you." Kimi stood.

She took the empty mugs and put them on the countertop. She poured a small amount of the hot water in each and then turned back to her grandfather. She leaned over and gave him a quick kiss on his forehead.

"I won't be long."

Niail went outside and waited for her to join him. He surveyed the area, noting the most likely place a potential threat would come from. The aspens hid the cabin from view. The only way in was a dirt track. That gave him pause. There was no clear sight line from the cabin. He reached for his gun just as Kimi opened the door.

"I hate those things."

"They're primitive." Niail shoved it back into the waistband of his jeans. "It is a necessary item on this planet."

"I wish it wasn't." Kimi sighed and started to walk away from the cabin. "We're at peace and we have people shooting at us. The law should be protecting us, yet we have an FBI agent and a drug dealer trying to kill us."

"Justice is never easy." Niail followed Kimi. His eyes continued to sweep the area. "That is why Hunters are needed."

"You seek justice?"

"We exist so that others may enact their own justice." Niail moved toward the trees along the side of the cabin. "The only reward for us is an honorable death."

Kimi stopped. "That's crazy. Everyone has something they look forward to."

Niail squinted to block the sun from his eyes. She was beautiful. Her body vibrated with outrage. The sudden urge to pull her close and ease her anger was overwhelming. He could not forget who he was though.

His expertise as a warrior was exceptional, even for clan Giath. Members of clan Giath were front line soldiers, skilled in marksmanship and storming the enemy. The fact that he had lived longer than most in his clan, spoke to his ability. Now he was faced with a new threat. Kimi.

The scent of her drew him near.

The feel of her seduced him.

Hunters had been denied the normal life of men by the use of enhancers and implants. Still, their legends spoke of such attraction. Niail was an experienced warrior, slow to change his ways. Unable to mind connect he could not seek the counsel of his fellow warriors. He was cast adrift. Forsaken.

His anchor now was Kimi.

Her safety was his mission.

"We are not like others." Niail chose his words with care. "There is only our brotherhood."

"So instead of wives and children they become your family."

"Yes."

"You can't believe they've abandoned you." Kimi frowned. "From everything you've told me they would be searching for you."

"It is not that simple."

Niail took a deep breath. The knowledge of mind connection was only known to Hunters and their mates. Kimi was his pair bond. He was certain even without being able to mind connect with her.

"Explain it then." Kimi touched his arm. "You are important to me. I need to understand."

"There is something I have not told you." Niail straightened his shoulders. "My injuries have made me incomplete."

Kimi's eyes searched his face. Her hand reached out to his head, her fingers feathering across the healing gash that Kowal's men had inflicted. She then moved down, caressing his chest before capturing his hands. Peace settled inside of him.

"Tell me."

"We are connected in ways that humans are not." Niail brought her hands up to his mouth and kissed them. "Remember our talk of pair bonds?"

Kimi nodded. "You form an intense bond that interferes with your ability to follow orders."

"We bond with only one woman." Niail's voice was low. "This bond is more than just physical."

Kimi frowned. "You said something about that before. Is there some strange alien ritual you haven't told me about?"

Niail smiled. She was beautiful. He would never tire of looking at her. She defended him to her brother and grandfather even though she had her doubts.

"I told you that a pair bond may refuse to mate." Niail's voice was low. "But he will be forever bonded. Her thoughts and desires will be his."

Niail waited for Kimi to speak. She bit her lip and looked away from him for a few seconds and then back. "So if she denies the bonding then he will suffer forever?"

"Never." Niail brushed a strand of hair from Kimi's face. "They can bond without being mated. We can connect with our brothers in the same way."

Kimi tilted her head. "Are you incomplete because your ability to unite is not working?"

Niail's gaze was fixed on Kimi. She had shown him that she could be trusted. Now he had to have faith in his instinct. She needed to know what they were facing. That was the honorable way.

"Yes." Niail cleared his throat. "All Hunters can mind connect with each other. A Hunter and his mate have the same linking."

"Are you talking about extra sensory perception?"

"What is that?"

Kimi shrugged. "I suppose it is using your mind to do things such as communicate or move objects. Sometimes it involves seeing the future or knowing where a person is."

"It is very specific with Hunters." Niail cleared his throat. "We communicate with each other with our thoughts, either all at once, or individually."

Kimi stared at him for several seconds before she shook her head. "You have your own built in cell phone. That's why you've been desperate to contact the others."

"There is only one reason for me to be silent and that is death."

Kimi gasped. "So they won't be looking for you."

"They have no reason to believe I am alive."

Niail watched Kimi as shock, disbelief, and then horror passed across her face. He sensed her emotions deep within his being also. It might not be a complete connection, but it was better than nothing.

Kimi took a deep breath. "Are you telling me that you can read your pair bond's thoughts also?"

"It works both ways." Niail took Kimi's arm and started to walk down the drive. "It is necessary for a Hunter to know if his mate is in trouble. That way he can protect her."

Kimi kept pace with him. "Can you read my thoughts? Is that why you think I'm your pair bond?"

"The hit on my head has made it impossible for me to mind connect." Niail leaned close to her.

"So you can't be certain."

"I sense your emotions and concerns." Niail's voice was firm. "I also know that you were worried by Mark's remarks about me and what I do."

Kimi's eyes widened. "Are you going to refute them?"

Niail caught the sight of a tire track out of the corner of his eye. He crouched down to examine it. There was no other. The hair on the back of his neck stood up. His eyes followed the track to where it turned around and then circled back along the dirt track that led to the cabin.

"Eight months ago we crashed on your planet." Niail's voice was steady, his gaze unwavering. "Since then we have found our way throughout North America. We have joined with others who were already on Earth. Our task is to give justice to those who cannot get it on their own."

"Are you some kind of vigilantes?" Kimi gave a choked laugh. "That's insane. Why would Kowal hire you to kill my brother?"

"He made the mistake of thinking he could fool us." Niail took Kimi's arm and started to walk with her to the cabin. "I can only surmise I uncovered his lies and that is why he tried to kill me."

"Thank goodness he wasn't successful."

Niail turned her to face him. "I need you to trust me. That is why I've told you what few humans know. It is imperative that no one else finds out about us."

Kimi's eyes roamed his face and then she nodded. "I'm not sure I believe all of it yet, but your secret is safe."

Niail nodded. It was done. He could not take back his words. She had protected him and given him time to heal. Her actions had shown courage. He would trust in that now.

He opened the door. The change in light forced him to squint and allow his eyes to adjust. When he could see, he walked to the table. Jake looked up.

"Anything new?"

"We must leave." Niail started to untie Mark. "There are tire tracks outside."

Jake rolled his eyes. "Grandfather just came in."

"These are single wheeled tracks."

"Is that important?" Kimi rubbed her arms.

"Motorcycle." Niail yanked Mark to his feet.

"It can't be Kowal. His men don't ride cycles." Jake's voice was a low hiss. "Who is it?"

"Does it matter?" Niail reached for Kimi's pack. "We need to leave now.

Chapter 13

Kimi's head ached. She had been trying to assimilate everything that Niail had told her. He had been matter of fact about his life. It even made sense when he had explained it. Deep down, she knew he thought she was his pair bond. She just couldn't see how that would fit in with her plans.

He wasn't Blackfeet.

Never mind that he was an alien.

What an alien, though. He was larger than most men. His muscles were well developed, and there wasn't an ounce of fat on his body. Any man who frequented a gym could be in the same shape. His physique did not mark him as an alien. He could easily pass for a human.

He had miraculous healing abilities.

The gash on the side of his head had been real. When Bobby had brought Niail to her, she hadn't thought he would live through the night. His body had been battered and bruised, and then there was the damage to his brain.

He had fallen from a truck and struck a boulder. People died from less. Bobby had been insistent that she not take him to a hospital. She had honored Bobby's wishes. After Niail's revelations, she was glad she had.

If he were an alien, the authorities would want to observe him. They would interrogate him. They might even do experiments on him. Niail would be lucky to be left alive.

If he weren't an alien, then he would be committed to the nearest mental institution. His delusions would ensure he was locked up for many years.

Neither scenario was good.

She shivered as she remembered his words about pair bonds and mating. He had been intense when he had told her. His eyes had never left her face while he spoke. She still thought that he was confusing gratitude with bonding. Her mind shied away from the possibility that he was right.

"How much farther?" Niail's voice interrupted her thoughts.

"Grandfather's directions said that we would have at least a one hour hike." Jake hitched his pack higher on his back. "We should have taken Mark to the nearest police station this morning."

"It was too risky." Niail took her arm and steadied her as she jumped over a small creek. "They had time to prepare for that."

"Kowal might still think Mark killed us."

"True, but he would have returned if that were the case."

Niail clasped her around the waist to help her over a fallen tree. A jolt of shock seared her body and for a second she contemplated leaning back and letting him wrap his arms around her. The heat of desire flickered deep inside, but she damped it down. She wasn't ready to have that kind of relationship.

"Enough, Jake." Kimi's voice was harsher than she had intended. "You and grandfather discussed all the options. You agreed to hike through these trails and skirt back onto the road. If anyone was watching the cabin, all they would see is Grandfather leaving in his truck."

"I didn't know how rough the terrain would be." Jake stopped and put his hands on his hips. "You can't tell me you're enjoying this?"

"I haven't enjoyed anything since the men broke into my house and started shooting."

Kimi pursed her lips. That wasn't strictly true. Jake had been a thorn in her side since he had started interfering in her life. It had begun when he had been suspended from the FBI. He had too much time on his hands. That's also when he had probably started to make a nuisance of himself with Kowal.

"Your interference in my life hasn't helped; especially your lectures concerning Sam."

"Your low-life ex isn't worth wasting breath on." Jake started walking again. "You're too soft. That's why I didn't want you seeing the man alone. I knew he would con you out of something and I was right."

"He couldn't afford to pay support."

Kimi wiped the sweat from her brow. She didn't have the energy to argue. She had moved on, and so had Sam. She had a good career. There was no reason not to sign the papers releasing him from his parental responsibilities.

"You shouldn't have let him off the hook." Jake spat the words at her. "He's their father. Just because he's started a new life and family, doesn't absolve him."

"He never sees the kids." Kimi grabbed Niail's arm as she teetered on some loose rocks. "This way I don't have to worry about his influence or demands."

"A man of honor remains with his family." Niail's voice was gruff.

Jake shrugged. "It's not right for two people to stay together when they detest each other."

"I never hated Sam."

"True." Jake shook his head. "You couldn't dislike anyone, but that only shows how poor your judgement is. Sam was useless."

"And now he's out of my life for good." Kimi blew the hair out of her eyes. "I made the right decision for me and the kids."

"We need to rest." Niail spoke in a stern voice.

"We don't have time." Jake stumbled forward.

"You are tired and your steps are unsure. Your arguments are illogical." Niail put his pack against a limber pine and brushed off a large boulder. "An amateur could follow us."

Kimi rolled her neck and massaged some of the kinks out with her hand. "I doubt anyone will want to traipse through here."

"You may be right. That means stopping will not be a problem." Niail led her to the rock. "Sit."

"Hey what about me?" Mark's voice was a loud whine.

"On the ground."

"You treat her like she's spun silk and me you just throw around." Mark struggled to sit with his hands tied in front of him. "That's no way to treat a prisoner. I'll probably get off for police brutality."

"I'm not the police. Your rules do not apply to me." Niail pushed Mark to the ground. "Women need protection and care. Men follow the orders."

"You really are from a different planet." Jake's eyes widened. "At the very least men and women are equal, although there are many who still believe that men are superior."

"They are wrong."

Niail pulled a bottle of water from his pack and handed it to Kimi. Her hand shook as she took it. She had the top unscrewed before it reached her mouth. The searing coolness soothed the gritty feeling in her mouth and throat. They had been walking non-stop for three-quarters of an hour. The sun was high in the sky and even though it was early June, its heat had her top soaked through with sweat.

"Kimi can barely keep up with us." Jake grinned as he accepted water from Niail. "She proves that women are the weaker sex."

"Women are more intelligent and compassionate then men." Niail held a water bottle up to Mark's mouth. "It is logical that they rule. It is the man's duty to protect and obey her."

Mark yanked the container out of Niail's grasp and held it up to his mouth with his bound hands.

Jake choked on a gulp of water. "You don't actually believe that?"

"It is the way of my world." Niail sat on the ground and raised his water to his lips. "It is who I am."

Jake stared at him for several seconds before shaking his head. He finished his water and then gathered the empty bottles. "I can hear a stream. I'll fill the bottles and put in the chlorine tablets." He was gone before anyone could stop him.

Kimi cleared her throat and looked at Niail. "Are there any problems between men and women where you're from?"

"Men obey, and women rule. How could there be problems."

"Don't the men want more?"

"There is honor in following the code." Niail leaned back against a pine. "As to the rest, I wouldn't know. I'm a warrior. I only have one purpose."

"To kill?" Kimi lowered her eyes.

"To serve."

Kimi glanced up with surprise. "That's a strange way to think of killing."

"A warrior serves his commanders." Niail's gaze swept over her before he looked away. "You should rest. There will be plenty of time for explanations later."

What a strange world he was from. Women ruled and men obeyed. Warriors had only one purpose. Hunters were denied love and a family because they wanted only one mate. It didn't seem possible that such a place could exist without conflict. Yet Niail spoke of it without emotion.

Jake returned fifteen minutes later. He looked at Niail

warily, almost as if he didn't believe he was real. The two men locked eyes. Kimi could have sworn that a silent understanding was reached. Jake picked up a pack and hitched it onto his back. He turned to Mark and yanked him to his feet.

"It's time to move."

Mark shook off his hand and sat back down. "This is abuse."

"You are alive." Niail threw the water bottles into his pack. "Men who betray do not deserve to live."

Mark spat on the ground. "It sounds like you're from a third world country without laws."

Niail spun around and grabbed Mark by the collar of his shirt and yanked him off the ground. "What good are laws if the people who should enforce them cheat?"

"Let me down." Mark struggled in Niail's hold. "You've no right to treat me like this."

"Be thankful I let you live." Niail threw him to the ground."

Mark glanced at Jake. "Are you going to let him talk to me like that?"

Jake shrugged. "You did break the law, and you cheated and betrayed me. If I wasn't sworn to protect, I might be inclined to let Niail have his way."

Niail straightened his shoulders. "He hinders our escape and his words irritate."

"True." Jake grinned. "But you agreed to do it my way."

"I will not go back on my word." Niail turned to Kimi. "Do you need help?"

She shook her head. "I'm right behind you. The sooner we reach the road the better."

"I think we were crazy to listen to Grandfather. Taking the car would have been so much easier." Jake looked down at the compass in his hand and then started off into the bush.

"He is an elder with much knowledge." Niail took up the rear. "He said he would meet us at the road."

They walked for another thirty minutes without finding the road. Kimi was wilting. She wiped her forehead on the bottom of her shirt and then squinted at the sun. It was high in the sky and was giving no relief from heat. They should have hit the road fifteen minutes ago and yet they still wandered in the bush. Her stomach growled and rumbled. They only had a few energy bars to last them until they found the road.

"I'm going on ahead."

Jake pushed through the overgrown juniper and was out of sight within seconds. Mark grunted and sat back against a tree. He was turned away from them.

"You need rest." Niail came to stand beside her. "We will find the road soon."

Kimi gave him a faint smile. "I think we're lost."

Niail shrugged. "When we have rested, I will discuss our location with Jake."

"He'll hate it if you prove him wrong."

"Why?"

"He likes to be right." Kimi wiped the sweat from the top of her lip. "Even as kids he was always the one who made up the rules. The rest of us followed."

"There is no sense in continuing in the wrong direction. No honor is lost by asking for help."

"Is everything about honor with you?"

"It is how I live." Niail pushed an aspen branch out of the way as he moved them into a small clearing. "I strive for honor in all that I do."

"So honor in fighting and honor in death?" Kimi raised an eyebrow. "That's not much of an existence."

Niail cleared his throat. "I have my brothers."

Kimi chest tightened at the intense loneliness he must be feeling. "When we get back to the town you must try and contact them on the computer to let them know where you are."

Niail nodded. "I will make certain you are safe first."

Kimi touched his arm. "I'm here for you."

Niail looked down at her. Her eyes widened at the intense emotion that she saw there. She was drowning in his gaze and she took a step closer. Naked desire flared in the depths of his dark eyes. He was going to kiss her.

Her heart sped.

Her breath caught in her throat.

His arm reached for her and pulled her close. She leaned into him, savoring the skittering sensations of excitement that spread out from where they touched. His head lowered. She lifted her mouth to meet his.

His tongue slid over her sealed lips. She shivered with need. Their tongues touched and curled together as the dance of passion began. The world spun away. There was only her and Niail.

A feather of sensation touched her mind and for a second they connected not only physically, but also mentally. She melted. He wove a spell that she could get lost in for a lifetime.

She wanted more.

Her arms reached about his neck and pulled him closer. Her fingers twined into his hair as liquid thrills of delight coursed through her veins. Hunger pulsed within her.

Jake's voice brought them back to earth. "I've found the road."

Niail eased his mouth away and cleared his throat. "Make certain the way is clear."

"Do you take me for a beginner?" Jake yelled as he

crashed toward them. "You can go first."

Niail heaved a sigh. He looked into her eyes and then released her. There was resignation and determination in his gaze now. She stepped back and watched him move past Jake. Their timing couldn't have been worse.

The attraction between them was insane. She was a woman with children. Men didn't want ready-made families, especially not when the responsibility included raising those children in the Blackfeet traditions.

She went to stand beside Jake. "I thought we were lost."

"Grandfather was off in his time, that's all." Jake put his compass back into his pocket. "You should rest while you can, sis. No telling if Grandfather will be in the right place or not. We'll probably have to walk to find him."

"Great." Mark rolled his eyes. "You guys haven't a clue what you're doing. I wouldn't be surprised if Kowal is waiting for you."

"That's why I sent Niail." Jake threw his pack on the ground. "He'll wipe the road with them."

"So now you believe all his warrior talk?" Kimi smiled and sat with her legs crossed.

"The man may talk crazy, but I've seen him fight." Jake leaned against a tree. "I've never seen skill like his before. I have to respect that."

"They are supposed to be the best when it comes to tracking and killing." Mark spoke in a hesitant voice. "I didn't believe it, but Kowal took it seriously enough. That's why he had his men inject him with a sedative before they started in on him. They thought he was dead for sure when they dumped him off the truck."

"He almost was." Kimi shivered as she remembered the condition he had been in when he was brought to her house. "What made Kowal attack him?"

Mark rested his chin on his knees. "It wasn't so much what he said, but his stance. He just stood there with his arms crossed."

"That's not enough of a reason to kill a man." Jake threw down a branch he had been stripping the leaves from. "He must have tried to attack you."

"No." Mark shrugged. "Kowal wasn't taking any chances. They're very explicit about lying. If they find that you've hired them under false pretenses, then they'll kill you."

Jake jerked his head away from the tree. "You said that before, but I didn't take it seriously."

"That's what the website says."

"Kowal must have been crazy to try and hire them." Jake shook his head. "I almost feel sorry for the man."

"Don't." Niail's voice interrupted them. "Kowal will pay for his lies."

Kimi looked up with a start. She hadn't heard his approach. The man must walk on air.

"I'm a law officer." Jake pulled Mark up. "I'll arrest you if you harm anyone, including Kowal."

"It is out of your hands." Niail crossed his arms over his chest. "Kowal made his choice. You are not responsible for him."

"I won't countenance murder."

"Justice will be served."

"Damn right, but the courts will decide the best course of action."

Niail only nodded and then turned to Kimi. "Will you be able to walk a bit longer?"

"Of course." Kimi stood. "Is Grandfather not there?"

"We are in the wrong place." Niail looked at Jake. "We will have to walk on the road."

"I followed the old man's directions." Jake picked up

his pack and started through the bush. "I'll bet you didn't look close enough."

"I was thorough." Niail pushed Mark ahead and then waited for Kimi.

When they arrived at the road there was no evidence of her grandfather's truck. They must be in the wrong place. Either that or her grandfather had been delayed. Kimi refused to consider what that might mean.

"We cannot stay in the open." Niail pushed Mark into the aspen trees lining the road and then turned to her. "Keep hidden."

"There is no way someone would be looking for us here." Jake stood at the road edge. "It'll be much easier to walk in the open."

"Your grandfather is not here." Niail turned a steady gaze to Jake. "Consider before you make any hasty decisions."

Jake looked up and down both sides of the clearing and then shrugged. "If you want to get bitten by bugs and clawed by branches, who am I to argue."

The muscle at the side of Niail's jaw tensed. "I will not risk Kimi's life for the sake of you saving face."

"She's my sister. I decide what is best for her."

Niail crossed his arms over his chest and stood looking at Jake. He didn't say anything, he just waited, letting the silence grow until Jake turned away. Kimi released the breath she had been holding and started to walk toward the bush. She was getting tired of the macho antics of these guys.

Niail came up to her. "I did not mean for you to be upset."

"I'm not." Kimi kept her voice curt.

"You think I am overly cautious." Niail touched her arm sending a shiver of delicious sensation up her spine.

Kimi heaved a sigh. "I understand, but must you and

Jake constantly fight over what you want to do. Jake is military trained and a police officer."

"I am skilled also." Niail's voice was low. "Your brother takes risks. He lets his emotions get in the way."

"He has always been a hot head, but the navy calmed him down."

"He is not ready to command."

"And you are?"

"I never expected to command, but compared to your brother, yes. I am ready to step in and lead this operation."

"He won't let you."

"I know."

Niail wasn't wrong. Her brother hadn't been thinking straight since he had found out his partner had betrayed their operation. Worse, Mark was on the payroll of a very bad group of men and Jake hadn't suspected anything. That must hurt his pride.

They had been walking about ten minutes when Niail held up a hand. "Quiet."

Kimi was too exhausted to argue. She stumbled to a stop and then sank down to the ground. She wiped her forehead and then pulled her water bottle out and took a deep drink. She strained her ears to hear, but other than the birds chirping, there was nothing.

"What?" Jake didn't hide his impatience.

"An engine." Niail pointed up the road. "About four hundred yards away."

"I don't hear anything." Jake shook his head. "You're on edge."

"No." Niail put his pack down and pulled out a couple of pistols. He checked the magazines and then snapped them back into place before putting them into his waistband. "We need to be ready."

Mark snickered. "You'll be sorry now."

Niail turned his eyes on their prisoner. "You were expecting this."

Mark shrugged. "There was always a possibility someone would catch up with us."

Before they had a chance to say anything else, there was the loud roaring noise of an engine coming toward them. Mark bolted for the road. He stumbled, but righted himself just as a truck skidded to a halt. There was a brute of a man behind the wheel. Another man with a scruffy beard was holding a gun to her grandfather's head.

Chapter 14

He should have followed his gut and went in the opposite direction. He had known Jake was totally messed up with their location. His head still felt like cotton wool, and his side ached, but that was no excuse. He had compromised their safety by not being more forceful with Jake.

He turned to Kimi and pointed to the trees. "Hide in there. I'll come for you when it's safe."

"What about you?" Kimi held her pack against her chest.

"I will be fine." Niail pulled out the two pistols and took the safeties off before turning to Jake. "You stay here. I need you to protect Kimi."

"I'm not missing the action." Jake bent over his pack for his pistol, but Niail wasn't waiting for him. He turned to the road and followed Mark.

None of this would have happened if they had dealt with Mark at the cabin. He should have killed Mark long ago. He was done with doing things by Jake's rules. The one thing a Hunter knew, was how to get out of a difficult situation.

He reached the road a few feet behind Mark.

"They're behind me," Mark shouted.

The man holding the gun on Kimi's grandfather pushed the older man down, and aimed his weapon at Niail.

A shot ripped past Niail's head. He didn't stop. He held both pistols in front of him and moved toward the truck. When he was within targeting distance he fired two shots. His aim was true.

He hit the men dead center in the forehead.

Then he turned his guns on Mark. "Halt."

Mark's fell to his knees beside the truck. He shook his head as he turned wide eyes to Niail. "No one is that good."

"What the hell?" Jake shouted from the edge of the dirt road. "You shot both of them."

"They would have killed us and your grandfather."

Jake walked to the vehicle. "How did these guys get here?"

"I think your partner can answer that."

Mark made a move toward a gun that had fallen out the truck window. Before he reached it, Niail shot the ground in front of him, spraying dirt up into his face. Mark scooted back on his bum, but Niail kept his gun trained on the traitor.

"Next time I will kill you."

"I'm not armed." Mark's voice was a high squeak. "You can't shoot me."

Niail bent and picked up the fallen pistol. "I do not follow your rules. Next time you die."

The truck door opened with a squeak and one of the dead men was pushed out. Eluwilussit jumped down and walked toward Niail. His step was slow. He shook his head when he reached him.

"I've never seen such accurate aim."

"I am clan Giath. We do not miss."

Eluwilussit nodded. "It's a good thing. Those men meant to kill all of us."

Jake stood in front of Eluwilussit with his arms crossed and legs spread. "How did they know where we were?"

Eluwilussit shrugged. "They showed up a few minutes after you left. They knew that you were with Mark."

They all looked over at Mark.

"How did you signal them?" Jake almost spit the words out.

"You're so predictable." Mark got to his feet. "When you said you were hiding on the reservation I knew it would be at your grandfather's cabin. I told Kowal where I would be if he didn't hear from me."

Jake's body tensed. "You disgust me."

"At least I have something to live for." Mark sneered. "All you have is your work. You don't even belong with your own people."

Jake took a step toward Mark, but Niail put out a restraining hand. "Enough. We either kill him now, or he arrives alive. There is no honor in hitting a man who cannot defend himself."

Jake threw off Niail's hand. "I can't believe you would say that after killing those men."

"It was necessary."

Jake stared at Niail for several seconds before throwing his hands up and turning away. "Put him in the back of the truck. Do you know how much paperwork I'll have to do to explain how these men ended up dead?"

"There is no reason to tell anyone." Niail picked up another discarded weapon. "We pull the bodies into the woods and the animals will take care of them."

"Do you do anything that is legal?"

"I follow the Sacred Code. Those are the only rules I need."

Niail put the weapons behind the truck seat. If Jake needed to explain their actions then that was his problem. He had no intention of being around when that happened. Once he got near a computer, he would report to his team leader. Partlan would know the best course of action.

He walked back into the bush at the side of the road. Kimi was still hiding, just as he had instructed. He could feel her fear. He needed to reassure her that everyone was safe.

When he reached the area where the backpacks were left, he called to her.

"Kimi."

There was no answer.

The panic he sensed seemed to mount.

"Kimi?" His voice was softer this time.

"What's the problem?" Jake spoke from behind him.

"Your sister is not answering." Niail pulled the pistol out of his waistband. "Something has frightened her."

"I'm sure all that gunfire didn't help." Jake picked up his pack. "I'm going back to the truck. I don't trust Mark with my grandfather."

Niail nodded. His attention was focused on Kimi. She was near, but he could not connect with her totally. His head was still too foggy for that. He felt her fear deep within his body, a twisting stab of terror. Had someone come at them from another angle and was now holding her captive? He hadn't considered that possibility when he had ordered her into hiding.

Gun ready, he started into the bush.

He zeroed in on her location.

She had not moved far from her original position. He kept his breathing steady and quiet as he pushed through the underbrush of junipers. He moved into the cool green shade of a cluster of aspens. Each step brought Kimi's anxiety into heart pounding focus.

Her fear grew worse with each step he took, until it was a relentless knot of anguish that twisted his gut.

He moved faster.

He pushed tree branches aside until she was within sight. Two men held her. Both had their pistols aimed at her head. Niail stopped. He took a deep breath and walked forward. He would need all of his training to get Kimi out of this situation alive.

"Forget something?" One of the men gave him a toothless grin. "We knew you would be back."

The other man stepped away from Kimi. His dark hair was greased back, and he had the cold, emotionless eyes of a killer. Niail had met his type before. His gun was now aimed at Niail.

"Put your weapon down or the girl gets it."

He took a deep breath and forced his heartbeat to slow. He could take out the man holding Kimi, but not without being hit himself. He would have to time his shots perfectly so that Kimi survived.

"Let her go." Niail dangled his gun between his thumb and index finger.

"We've learned a thing or two about you since our last meeting." The toothless guy spat on the ground. "We don't do nothing until that gun is out of your hands."

Niail dropped the pistol. "Release her."

"She's leverage." The other man took a step toward Niail. "You and me have unfinished business. I should have made certain you were dead before I dumped you on the road."

"A mistake you will regret."

"Well, you won't have to worry about that for much longer. This time I will return to Kowal with your dead body." The man grinned. "It's either that or the boss will kill me."

"You can have me. She goes free." Niail gestured to Kimi.

The cold one looked back at Kimi and shrugged. "I don't see a problem with that."

Kimi shook her head. "Go Niail. They'll kill me after you're dead anyways. Save yourself."

The man tightened his arm around her neck. She gasped, trying to get more air. He didn't release his hold. The chill of determination raced up Niail's spine. He tensed his muscles and prepared for death. He could get one bullet off before he would be hit. Then he would kill the second one.

"You want me." He took a step closer. "Take your shot now. You will not have a better opportunity."

The toothless one grinned and took his gun away from Kimi's head. Niail sent a wave of love to Kimi and then reached behind his back for his second pistol. He shot the man holding Kimi. He swung around to the second man just as the sound of another gun firing split the air.

Kimi screamed.

"Are there any others?" Niail turned to look at Jake.

Jake shook his head. "That was a hell of a chance you took. What if I hadn't been behind you?"

"I would have taken a bullet."

Niail pulled Kimi into his arms.

She sagged into his chest. Her body trembled and he pulled her tighter to try and ease the shivers of reaction that were flowing through her.

"So getting shot was part of your strategy." Jake bent down and picked up the gun from the man he had just killed. "That sounds like no plan at all."

"I am always prepared to die to keep those under my watch safe."

"That makes you some sort of glorified bodyguard then." Jake shook his head and went to pick up the weapon from the toothless guy. "If you use your bodies as shields then you guys don't plan on living long."

"No." Niail soothed his hand down Kimi's back. "I have lived more than most in my clan."

"I bet life insurance is expensive."

"What is insurance?"

Jake rolled his eyes. "It was a joke. Nobody in their right mind would give you coverage."

Jake used his foot to push the toothless guy over onto his back. "This is one of Kowal's men."

"They both are." Kimi looked at her brother. "They were talking about it before Niail found us."

Jake nodded. "I've seen them when I was doing surveillance. They're pretty high up in the organization."

"They meant to kill all of us." Kimi shivered. "They said we knew too much to let us live."

Niail turned to walk back to the road. He held Kimi close, sending her calming energy. Tremors still shook her body, but they had lessened in number and intensity.

"We have to do something with the bodies." Jake followed Niail to the road.

"Why?"

"It's indecent." Jake shook his head. "I have to report it to headquarters and get the coroner out here. Does nothing about the killings shake you up?"

"They are dead." Niail stopped when he reached the area where they had left their packs. He led Kimi to a tree and eased her down. She sighed and leaned her head against the white colored trunk. Her eyes were closed, but he sensed that she was fighting for control.

He turned back to Jake. "Where is Mark?"

"Grandfather tied him up at the truck." Jake grinned "He surprised me with how calm he was about the whole situation."

"He is a wise man." Niail picked up a pack. "I must thank you for coming to my aid."

"No problem." Jake handed him another pack. "I couldn't believe you planned to go it alone. Don't you guys know anything about buying time?"

Niail frowned. "Time is not for sale."

"It means giving someone else time to get there and help." Jake hiked a pack onto his back and started for the road. "Honestly, you're way too literal."

"He means well." Kimi's soft voice stopped Niail. "Thank you for saving me."

"I vowed to protect you and I will."

Niail held his hand out to Kimi. She clasped her fingers around his palm and a shock of awareness bolted up his arm. It was a welcomed sensation.

Kimi must have felt it too because her eyes widened. She tightened her hand about his and looked up at him. "You feel it too."

"Our bond is strengthening."

Kimi tilted her head. "Couldn't it just be sexual attraction?"

"Not for me." Niail pulled Kimi up so that she was standing within the circle of his arms. "I no longer have any doubts. You are my pair bond. The one woman destined to be my mate."

Chapter 15

For a brief second Kimi wanted to agree with Niail, but then the reality of their situation hit her. There was no denying she was attracted to Niail. He made her feel sensations that she had long thought dead, if they had ever been alive. There were a couple of problems.

He was an alien.

Worse, he was a trained killer.

Many men were trained to kill in the line of duty, but it was different for Niail. He was single-minded in his approach. He didn't hesitate to kill a person if they were a risk to those he was protecting. He lived by a code that allowed and encouraged this behavior. This was not even morally similar to her beliefs.

She lived in the Blackfeet tradition.

All life was sacred to her.

She believed in her Grandfather's teachings and medicine. All she asked from life was to have a safe and secure home to raise her children in the traditional ways. Since Niail had come into her life, nothing had been safe or secure.

"I can see my words have upset you."

Kimi shook her head. "You're not used to being close to women and I think you've mistaken attraction for something deeper."

"My implants were removed months ago." Niail lowered his voice. "In none of that time have I felt the least bit drawn to another woman."

"Why me?" Kimi's breath caught at the intensity of Niail's gaze.

"I cannot explain why we were chosen to be as one." Niail reached for her, his hands soothing over her arms. "I just know that I will never mate with another woman. You are my pair bond."

"I'm not ready for that kind of commitment." Kimi's voice shook. "We've just met. I swore I would never become involved with a man who didn't believe in the same traditions as me. You're not Blackfeet."

Niail grinned. "I am not human either, but that does not change how I feel. We are bonded."

Kimi pushed away. "This is too much for me to deal with right now."

"There is nothing to concern you." Niail reached for her arm and started leading her to the road. "I am bonded with you. The longer we stay together, the closer our connection will be."

"And I have no say?"

"You can refuse the bond and the mating." Niail pushed a branch clear of the path. "I will honor your decision."

"Then what happens?"

"If you do not want the bond, then I will not be able to link with you."

Kimi's eyes narrowed. "Connect through our thoughts?"

"Yes." Niail stopped walking and turned to her. "When those men were holding you I knew that you were afraid. I knew there was danger."

"So you'll always know when I'm in danger?"

"Yes."

Kimi bit her lip. It seemed like a good thing. If Niail knew when she was in peril, then he could help. There didn't seem to be a down side to it, especially given the situation they were in right now.

"That's all?" Kimi took a deep breath. "You won't be expecting anything else from me?"

"You can trust me." Niail stepped out onto the road. "I will honor your decision."

Kimi nodded. "Then I suppose the sensible thing would be to see what happens after we're out of danger. If there is still some connection, then we can explore what to do about it then."

"As you wish." Niail waited until she was beside him. "Know that I will always protect you whether you agree to be my mate or not. The pair bond is real."

She heaved a sigh. "I still think you'll change your mind about that. For now, let's get to safety."

Niail clasped her arm and a thrill raced through her. Whatever this attraction was, it was powerful. All she wanted was to sink into his arms and surrender. It was irresistible. She would have to be careful not to fall under its spell because she had no intention of uprooting her life.

"Hurry." Jake motioned them toward the truck. "I need to get to my contact's house. He'll know the best course of action."

Niail threw the packs into the truck's box. Then he clasped her waist and lifted her onto the cab's bench seat. She scooted past the steering wheel and moved to the far door. When Kimi was settled, her Grandfather positioned himself on the driver's side. Niail and Jake jumped into the open back of the truck. Mark was already in the box, with his hands cuffed to a tie down.

Her grandfather turned the key and put the pickup in gear. "We'll stop at the cabin and pick up the other vehicles."

Kimi clasped her hands in her lap. Niail's words from earlier were spinning in her head. His talk of pair bonds and mating was foreign to her. Her stomach churned with indecision. She didn't want her life turned upside down.

She turned to her Grandfather. "What do you think about Niail?"

"He is a man to be trusted." The vehicle jolted and sputtered.

"But he kills."

Her grandfather shifted gears and the truck started to run smoother. "He protects. He is a man of honor."

"He thinks I'm his mate." The words were out of her mouth before she had a chance to think.

"What do you believe?"

"If he's a Star Person, then he's not from earth." Kimi's voice wavered. "That means he's an alien."

"That doesn't make him a lesser man." Her grandfather gave her a sideways glance. "I've noticed you are not indifferent to him."

Kimi frowned. "There's a strange energy that pulses through me when he's near, or touches me. He calls it pair bonding. Niail believes that when the bonding strengthens, he will always know when I'm in danger."

"Your brother says he was willing to take a bullet for you."

"He has promised to guard me." Kimi wrung her hands. "I can't let him continue to do that, especially when I don't know how I feel about him."

"It's what he wishes." Her grandfather frowned. "You're at risk. Why would you deny his protection?"

"I can't promise to return his affection."

Kimi knew she sounded indecisive, but she couldn't help it. As much as Niail said he didn't want anything in return, her experience of men had taught her differently. She refused to be indebted to any man. It always led to hurt feelings, and disappointment.

"It seems you already care." Her grandfather's tone was dry.

"He's not Blackfeet." Kimi's voice was tinted with sadness. "I vowed after Sam that if I let another man into my life, he would have to share our traditions."

"You search for perfection." Her grandfather tilted his head at her. "You won't find it in this world."

"I couldn't bear to be hurt again."

"There is no remedy for that." Her grandfather sighed. "You're grandmother left this earth when I was still a young man. There has been no healing the hole she left in my heart. To love is to grieve."

"Then why chance it?"

"The joy and beauty of love is never forgotten." Grandfather smiled, his face softened by memories. "That is worth the pain."

"I want the children raised in our traditions." Kimi glanced out the side window. "Niail's beliefs are so different. I don't think he would be a good influence."

"You are making excuses." Her grandfather's voice was stern. "Do not forget the legend of the choosing of mates. Chief Woman disguised herself as a beggar woman and chose Old Man as her mate. He refused to go with her because she looked old and poor. After all the other women had chosen mates, she came out as herself, and Old Man did everything he could to make her pick him, but she chose another. Old Man was left without a mate and Chief Woman turned him into a pine tree."

Kimi smiled. She had heard this tale many times. "Are you suggesting I'll end up a tree?"

"You should not judge Niail by what you see." Grandfather turned into the drive for the cabin. "You may find yourself alone. Trust me, time moves slow when there is no one to share it with."

The truck came to a stop in front of the cabin. Kimi looked over at her grandfather and nodded. "Thank you."

"You let your mind dwell on the things that don't matter." Her grandfather put his hands over hers. "Let you heart lead you in this."

"I'll try."

At that moment Niail pulled the door open. "We must not delay."

Kimi jumped down and started toward the cabin. The sooner they got on the road, the better. She knew that Ann would be taking care of the children, but she wanted her life back to normal. That wasn't going to happen until Jake contacted his superiors.

Jake was ahead of her and he ran behind the cabin. Their vehicles should still be there. Kimi leaned against the cabin door and waited for her grandfather and Niail to reach her. She was exhausted emotionally and physically. Too much had happened. Her mind was churning with everything that Niail had told her. Grandfather was right. She needed to stop thinking and let her heart lead her.

Her grandfather opened the door and Kimi stumbled in behind the men. She headed for the couch and sank into it with a sigh.

"You need rest." Niail stood behind the couch.

"You're the one injured." Kimi settled her head into the backrest. "Let me know when the vehicles are ready. I'll be happy when these guys are arrested and I can sleep in my own bed."

"That's not happening for a while." Jake stood at the cabin door.

Kimi straightened up and looked at him. He was out of breath, and his eyes were darting around the cabin. Before she could speak, Niail had pushed past Jake and gone outside.

"What happened?"

"They've vandalized the vehicles." Jake pulled a chair out and sat. "The tires are slashed."

"Can we fix them?"

Jake shook his head. "We only have two spare tires between the vehicles."

Niail came back into the cabin. "We will all have to leave in your grandfather's truck."

Grandfather had gathered his pack of supplies and put it on the table. "I will drive you."

"Sooner would be best." Niail grabbed the pack off the table. "There is no sign of the dead men's vehicle so we have to assume they were dropped off by someone. That means they will return when the men we have killed do not show up."

Jake heaved a sigh and stood. "I forgot about that. We should go to Andrew's house. He's my supervisor and no one will expect us to meet up with him there."

Kimi sighed and pushed off the couch. There would be plenty of time to rest later. All that matter now was getting to safety. She joined Niail at the door and he pulled her close. She inhaled his scent and instantly felt energized.

"It will be over soon." Niail led her to the truck.

When she was seated, he shut the door and jumped into the back. She turned and looked at him, her gaze never leaving his face. A sense of comfort and safety infused her body.

This was a man who could possess her totally. With a start she realized that was exactly what she wanted; to be utterly and completely part of Niail. She ached for him. She wanted his words about pair bonding to be true. She needed to know that she was as much a part of him as he was of her.

A flame flickered deep within Niail's eyes and she knew. No words were needed. He had sensed her thoughts. She didn't know how, but he had reached deep within her.

Somehow he had captured the part of her that was scared and frightened and was soothing it. His protection surrounded and comforted her.

The spell was broken when her grandfather opened his door and sat behind the wheel. Kimi sighed and turned away from Niail. Once they were safe, there would be time to explore the sensations that were racing through her. Now she must focus on getting help from the police. She needed her life to get back to normal.

The drive to town was accomplished in silence. Her grandfather was a man of few words and Kimi knew that he had said all he meant to about her relationship with Niail. Grandfather saw no reason for them not to be together. That was all he was going to say about the matter.

They arrived in Cut Bank just after dark. They drove down Main Street and turned off past the County Building until they came to a residential area. He stopped in front of a small beige clapboard sided house. Jake jumped down and unlocked Mark from the tie down.

"I'll contact the head of the department from here and see what he wants me to do. Hopefully we can get a police van sent to transport Mark to Billings. I would feel safer that way. I don't know how far reaching Kowal's control is."

Grandfather turned the vehicle off and jumped out. "I will come with you. I need to stretch my legs."

Niail opened the truck door beside Kimi. "Are you certain you can trust this man?"

"He's law enforcement and my contact in the area." Jake's tone was impatient. "You see conspiracy around every corner."

"No." Niail rested his arm on the vehicle's door. "I have seen more corruption than you. I have also cleaned up more messes."

Mark snickered. "Nothing is as it seems."

Jake gave him a shake. "Enough. There's no doubt of your guilt. If you had your way we would all be dead."

"All we wanted was the Hunter. Remember that." Mark pulled against Jake's lead. "Now it's probably too late."

A shiver raced up Kimi's spine. Niail glanced down at her and she forced a smile. The thought of someone taking Niail away was painful. She would barely be able to handle it when he returned to his own kind. At least then she would know he was safe.

"I will never leave you."

Kimi's eyes widened. How had he known what she was thinking? He'd said his brain was too confused to read thoughts.

Niail leaned close. His breath tickled her ear. "Our bond is strengthening. My head is unclear of everything, but you."

"That's not possible." Kimi's words were a whisper.

"It is possible for a Hunter."

Kimi bit her lip, her eyes glancing from side to side. "Can you read everyone's mind?"

"I hear only your thoughts."

Kimi exhaled. "As long as you're the only one."

"Not everything is clear, but as the bond grows I will know more and more of your desires."

Kimi's tongue skittered across her lips. Niail's words had sent a thrilling heat through her. His gaze was intense, his voice low, and somehow she knew that to have this man's attention would be heavenly. Still, she couldn't allow herself to forget that she was a mother with children to look out for.

Niail bent closer, his lips a hair's breadth away. Kimi's breath caught in her throat, anticipation heightened as she waited for his touch. His lips skimmed hers and she moaned as he moved away. His mouth returned, this time he captured her lips with deftness and firmness. She gasped at the electric sensation that raced through her. His tongue delved into her mouth. He drank from her, sending shivers of delight throughout her. She reached her arms up to his neck and pulled him closer. Everything disappeared. All that mattered was Niail and the pleasure he was sending throughout her body. She pressed closer to him, craving for a deeper connection.

Her head spun with the dizzy thrill of ecstasy. She was lost. She surrendered to the passion and joy of being with him. Their kiss deepened until she felt part of him.

They were one.

She needed more.

She ached to be joined with him, to feel his body next to hers. He was all that existed. The world vanished except the exquisite passion that was building within her. She was lost to everything except Niail.

The blast of a shotgun tore them apart.

Chapter 16

Every cell in Niail's body jumped into protection mode. For a few minutes he had lost himself in the feel and taste of Kimi. He had let himself forget the danger they were in. He should not have listened to Jake. His instincts had warned him it was not safe. He pushed Kimi down flat on the seat.

"Stay."

He locked and shut the door before running to the house. The nondescript building looked non-threatening, but that gunshot had been close. Niail flattened his body against the side wall and then inched his head out so he could see the front porch.

There was no sign of Jake or Mark. Eluwilussit was hurrying toward him, though. When he spotted Niail he ran to his side and leaned against the wall. His breath was coming in gasps and he put his hand to his chest.

"What happened?" Niail's voice was low.

Grandfather shook his head. "I was outside the door. I didn't see anything."

"So we do not know if Jake is okay?" Niail reached behind and pulled a handgun out of his waistband.

"You can't go in there." Grandfather's voice rose. "They're armed."

"I cannot leave Jake to fight alone." Niail pushed the safety off his weapon. "He has shown himself to be a man of honor. You need to go back to the truck. I left Kimi there."

"I'll start the vehicle and have it running just in case you need a quick escape."

Niail nodded. "Good. If we are not out in five minutes, you are to leave. Kimi needs to get to safety."

Niail didn't wait for Eluwilussit's agreement. He steadied his breathing and then slipped around the edge of the wall. He kept his body flat against the building and took short side steps until he was at the front door.

The door was wooden with a glass upper section. There was a bullet hole in the bottom corner of the window. Around the hole was an area of shattered glass with spiral cracks extending from it in on all sides. The shot had come from inside the house.

Niail's grip on the handgun tightened.

He inhaled and kicked the door open in one motion.

He ducked low and rushed to the nearest wall for cover. In the hallway, near the door, was a dead body. It was male. Niail had never seen him before, so he assumed it was Jake's contact.

Bullets whizzed by his head.

He counted three.

He eased along the wall. When he reached the corner he took several steadying breaths. Once his heart rate was lowered, he peered around the edge. Three men had surrounded Jake. One had a gun to his head. The other two were pointing in his direction. Mark was nowhere in sight.

"We've got your buddy," one of the men yelled. "We'll let him live if you give yourself up."

"Don't believe them." Jake's voice was defiant. "They've already killed Andrew."

Niail pulled back just as two bullets flew by. A third one embedded in the wall behind his head. He crouched down on his knees, keeping the gun in front of him. He cocked his pistol and leveled it at the corner.

He closed his eyes and envisioned the position of the men. He reached out with his senses and focused on the different cadence of each man's breathing. He exhaled and steadied his hand before jumping from behind the wall. He pulled the trigger three times as he rolled side over side, to the opposite wall.

"Damn." There was a tremor in Jake's voice. "You were dead center in the forehead for all three."

Niail eased around the edge of the corner. The men were lying on the floor and Jake was standing. His eyes scanned the room for Mark. There was no sign of him.

"I do not miss." Niail pulled the magazine from his 9mm and checked the number of bullets. He still had ten left.

"Where is he?"

"Mark?"

"Is there more than him?"

"He's the only one left. He ran out the back door the minute you entered the house."

Niail stood and leaned against the wall. He eased his breathing and wiped the beads of sweat from his head. He glanced around the corner. Jake had picked his way around the bodies and was coming toward him.

"How did you do that?" Jake's voice was hoarse. "Can you see through walls?"

"No." Niail moved into the room. "This planet gives us increased abilities. My hearing is better, so I used that to locate you before shooting."

"Incredible. You could've hit me."

Niail shrugged. He could hear the anxiety in Jake's voice. It was a waste of energy. He had not missed. Now they had to focus on what to do next. As long as Mark and Kowal were free, Kimi was in danger.

"What happened here?"

"Mark knew these guys were staking out Andrew's place." Jake bent down and with a shaking hand he picked up a pistol. "As soon as we were inside, the men barged in from the rear. They killed Andrew before I knew what was happening."

"Your partner is not a man we should let live."

Jake lowered his eyes. "Perhaps not, but he is a witness to what happened to you. He knows Kowal's operation. I want him alive."

Niail's eyes narrowed. How many times did Jake have to see the error of his choices? Humans might think that they were being fair by letting a man stand his trial, but where was the honor in this? Mark was a traitor who had knowingly allowed innocent people to die. He was a coward.

"You are only delaying the inevitable."

Jake shook his head. "There will be more justice if Mark pays for his behavior."

"Death is a payment."

"Not in this case." Jake picked up a second pistol. "He has to testify to what these men have done."

Niail heaved a sigh. "It is your decision."

He walked past the dead men on the floor and went through a passageway that led to the kitchen. There was an open door to the outside. Now he needed to track his prey. He paused at the doorway and sniffed the air. The stench of body odor assailed his nostrils.

Mark was nearby.

Niail's eyes scanned the darkness.

A shadow moved to the right, but it was too small to be his prey. He took a step forward and the stillness of the night closed in upon him. A jolt of cold skittered up his spine. Instinct and experience, told him that Mark waited close by. The sound of a dog barking in the distance broke the silence.

He took another step forward.

The nightscape seemed to have eyes that peered deep within him. A sharp cracking sound came from the left. Niail tilted his ear in that direction. A soft rustle, and then a sigh alerted him to his quarry. Niail eased his gun up.

He bent low and moved on silent feet, inching his way into the darkness. Mark was there. He could feel and smell him. When he reached a stone edging, he stepped over it onto a gravel path. A soft crunch of stone reverberated in his head. He lightened his footstep as he turned in direction of the sound.

A shadow swooped from nearby and Niail ducked. He wasn't quick enough to prevent the blow to the head. He staggered back several steps as the cold metal of a gun cracked against his skull. Niail winced at the tooth jarring pain that shot through him. He pushed past it and grabbed the arm that wielded the weapon.

"Let go." Mark screamed in pain.

Niail twisted the arm back. "Release the gun."

"Never."

Niail grunted and put the full weight of his body behind the force of his hold. He was within seconds of breaking the arm, when Mark relented.

"Stop." The clatter of metal on the gravel followed.

Niail released Mark's arm and then pulled back his fist and punched him in the jaw. Mark's body slumped to the ground just as Jake ran up.

"What did you do to him?" Jake's words came out between his gasps for air.

Niail hauled Mark to his feet. "You can thank me later."

He shoved his prisoner ahead of him as they moved back to the house. Instead of entering the back door, Niail pulled Mark around the side of the building. The truck was still there and running just as Eluwilussit had promised.

Jake took Mark from Niail and cuffed his hands.

"He almost broke my arm." Mark's voice was a high pitched whine. "You'll never be able to try my case in court. You'll be arrested for brutality."

The door opened and Kimi came rushing to their side. "What happened?"

"They were watching the house." Jake dropped the tailgate and pushed Mark up onto the truck bed. "One minute I'm talking to Andrew and telling him about the operation and the next he's dead."

"How horrible." Kimi's voice shook.

"Your sister does not need to hear this." Niail leaned against the side of the vehicle. His head ached. He clenched his jaw and pushed back the pain.

Kimi turned to him. "Are you okay?"

Niail straightened away from the truck. "Mark put up a fight."

"I clocked him good." Mark chuckled. "He's not so tough."

Kimi inhaled a deep breath. "Where did he hit you?"

"My head."

Kimi reached up and brushed the hair from his forehead. Her hand feathered across the spot where Mark had bashed him. He winced and had to force himself not to move away from her. Her caress was soothing. Never had anyone cared about his injuries before. It was a unique sensation.

"You're bleeding." Kimi pulled him along with her to the front of the truck. "Let me have a better look."

She flicked the interior light on and pushed him toward the light. She frowned as her fingers moved his hair aside and revealed the open gash a few inches above his temple.

"You need stitches."

"There is no time." Niail winced as he straightened up.

"He's right." Jake spoke from the rear of the truck. "We need to get you to safety and then I'm going straight to Billings."

"You thought it would be safe here." Kimi's voice was sarcastic.

"I was wrong." Jake put his hands on his hips. "I think you should go back to your house, gather a few things, and then find someplace to hide. They've already been to your place, so it's not likely they'll return."

"You can't be certain."

"Well I can't take you to Billings." Jake crossed his arms over his chest. "There isn't enough room in the truck."

Kimi looked over at Niail with a raised eyebrow. A rush of warmth went through him at her silent question. She was looking to him for direction. She trusted him enough to want his input.

"I will not leave you." Niail touched her arm. "You will be safe."

"Are you certain?" Kimi looked at his forehead. "We should get you stitches first."

"I am fine."

Niail helped Kimi back into the truck and shut the door. He hopped into the back and braced himself against the side. His head was pounding and his stomach rolled with nausea, but that was not going to stop him from staying close to Kimi. She needed him.

The trip to Kimi's house took almost half an hour. By the end of the journey Niail didn't care where they stopped, so long as they did. His head throbbed, and his eyes were going in and out of focus. For the last fifteen minutes of the trip he had held his head in his hands and used visualization techniques to push the pain away. No interrogation had given him this much agony.

The truck pulled up to Kimi's house. The lights were out and everything was an inky dark color. Niail jumped down and went to the passenger door. He clasped Kimi's waist and helped her out of the vehicle before turning to the house.

The hair on the back of his neck stood up.

Everything looked in place, but his senses told him something was wrong.

He halted Kimi. "Let me go first."

"What now?" Kimi's voice was weary. "I just want to call Ann and make sure the kids are okay. Maybe we could stay here the night. I would love to fall asleep in my own bed."

"Not going to happen." Jake was pushing Mark in front of him. "After you check on the kids and freshen up, I want you out of here."

"But you said they wouldn't come back here."

Jake motioned to the house. "This place is too isolated, even with the superhero taking care of you. Your truck is still at Grandfather's, so you have no way of leaving."

Kimi groaned. "Will I get any sleep tonight?"

"Sure, as long as it's some place where Kowal's men can't get you." Jake moved Mark toward the house. "Once I've got the police working on this, they'll need to speak to you.

Kimi put her hand over a yawn. "I hate to think how Niail feels."

"I do not stop until the job is done."

"Listen to him. He knows what's best."

Niail shook his head. "I will not go to the police. It is too dangerous for me."

Eluwilussit who had been walking behind them spoke now. "He must stay hidden."

"He can't use the Star People as a defense." Jake stopped and turned to face Niail. "You killed people. Even if it's in self-defence it must be reported."

"It is not wise for me to be involved."

"You just admitted the job isn't done."

"I still have to kill Kowal." Niail led Kimi forward.

"Let the police handle it now." Jake grabbed Niail's arm and spun him around. "If you take the law into your own hands, then I'll have to arrest you."

"You can try."

"Don't threaten me." Jake almost spit his words. "This is not a joke. I don't care where you're from, in my country you have to follow the rules."

"I follow the Sacred Code."

Niail had reached the door. He sniffed the air and then tensed. His stomach knotted and he pushed Kimi behind him. All his senses warned him of danger.

There was someone in the house.

He wanted Kimi out of the line of fire. He pulled his pistol from his waistband and readied for battle. He took the keys from Kimi and unlocked the door.

"Go back to the truck." His voice was a low whisper.

Jake raised an eyebrow and then handed Mark over to Eluwilussit. He motioned his grandfather to follow Kimi. When they had left, Niail pushed the door open with his foot and then moved to the side of the doorway. Jake followed his lead and went to the other side.

Silence greeted them.

Niail nodded to Jake and then he stepped into the house. He crouched low. Jake ran into the room, but before he had gone more than two feet an arm came out and knocked him back to the floor.

Niail's hand that held his gun was hit from the side. His pistol was sent flying across the floor. He grabbed the leg of his assailant, but a deep chuckle stopped him.

Chapter 17

Partlan.

He was a fellow Hunter and his team leader.

Niail sagged against the door jamb and grinned. "It's about time you found me."

"You are the one who kept moving." Partlan reached a hand down and pulled Niail up.

"It was either that or be killed." Niail motioned for Kimi and Eluwilussit to come in. "Here is the woman who took me in."

Kimi moved to a propane light fixture beside the door. She turned the knob on the lamp and held a match to it. Light flooded the area. Then she moved to stand beside Niail.

"Kimi, this is Partlan. He is an excellent warrior of the clan Obair."

Kimi shook Partlan's hand and then turned to the rest of the men that he was introducing her to. "This is Ranon, Turlo, Malac, and Gur."

Niail turned to Jake and Eluwilussit. "This is Kimi's brother, Jake, and grandfather Eluwilussit."

Jake was brushing himself off. "Where is Mark?"

"I locked him in the car." Eluwilussit spoke in an unhurried voice. "He tried to run away so I tied him to the steering wheel."

Partlan turned to the older man. "He is your prisoner?"

When Eluwilussit nodded, Partlan continued, "A wise move."

They went into the kitchen where Kimi lit two more propane lamps on the wall. Light flooded the small room. The mugs from the previous day were on the sink board and the table had a few napkins spread over it. Other than that, there was no obvious evidence that Kowal's men had almost killed them here the previous night.

Ranon pushed Niail into a chair. "You took Niail in?"

Kimi nodded. "Bobby brought him to me when he was thrown from a truck. He had a huge gash on his head and a concussion. That first night I didn't think he would make it."

Partlan crossed his arms over his chest. "He is the unit's best shot and one of our most experienced warriors."

A flicker of pride seared through Niail. Praise was seldom given or needed. Doing one's duty was tribute enough, yet it was good to know his brothers thought him useful. Ranon pulled out a small light and started flashing it at his eyes. He blinked and tried to move away from its intense beam.

Then Ranon started to examine him, stopping for a few seconds at the wound in his side. He shook his head and then pulled out some dressings from his case. Within seconds he had poured antiseptic onto his cuts and put a new dressing on his side.

He took longer with the fresh gash on his head. Niail inhaled as another cleansing agent was poured over the area. He clenched his jaw in readiness as he watched Ranon pull a suture kit from his bag. He felt the skin pulled together and the sharp prick of the needle as each edge was sewn closed. When Ranon had finished he covered it with a bandage. Then he stepped back.

"Well?" Partlan's voice was short. "Why can we not communicate?"

"He still has the after effects of a concussion." Ranon shook his head. "There is no telling how long that will last. He may never be able to connect again."

The news hit Niail like a blow to his heart. To never mind connect with the others? That was signing his death warrant. To be cut off from his brothers and to be useless in a battle, was not acceptable.

"There must be something you can do." Niail jerked back in the chair. "I have to get better."

"Time and rest are the only things that will heal your head." Ranon sighed. "Unfortunately it does not look as if you have rested."

"Kowal's men have been trying to kill us." Jake cleared his throat. "What's the problem with communication? I know the cell phone connections aren't reliable out here, but when you're closer to town there should be a signal."

"Niail is still having headaches." A surge of warmth went through Niail as Kimi put her hand on his shoulder. "He says his head feels foggy. Could that be part of his problem?"

Ranon pursed his lips. "It will not help him."

"He also can't remember anything about his accident." Kimi's fingers soothed him.

"That is not unusual with a concussion." Ranon leaned toward him. "I am sorry my news is not better."

"I appreciate you coming to help." Niail gave Partlan a quick glance. "I did not wish you to be concerned."

Partlan nodded. "Silence usually means death. We cannot lose any more brothers."

"I tried to find another way to contact, but things happened fast and this place is remote. There is no Internet. By the time I reached a phone, the number was disconnected."

At that moment there was a loud crash and then the door burst open. Mark stood in the doorway, a gun in his hands. His eyes widened when he saw the other Hunters and then he aimed his weapon toward Kimi.

"She's coming with me." He waved the gun at her. "Move."

Kimi sighed. Before she could take a step Niail stood and pushed her behind him. At the same time Partlan and Turlo moved on Mark. Partlan grabbed the hand that held the weapon and pushed it into Mark's ribs. The reflexive action of Mark's finger on the trigger fired the pistol.

Mark's eyes widened and then glazed over before he sagged against the wall. Partlan held the man in place until the last breath passed through Mark. When death was certain he moved the body outside.

Partlan stepped back inside and closed the door behind him.

"You just shot a police officer." Jake's voice wavered.

"He threatened a woman." Partlan eye's locked with Jake's. "We defend women and children above all else. I do not ask questions when that happens. I act."

"You could have disarmed him."

"Why? He had no honor." Partlan's voice was devoid of emotion. "There is no point in sparing such a person."

"You guys are seriously deranged." Jake looked around at the other warriors. They stood there with arms crossed and faces impassive.

Partlan looked at Niail. "It is best if you do not come on this mission. We will return once Kowal is dealt with."

Niail nodded. "Yes."

"What mission?" Jake stood in front of Partlan. "This is my jurisdiction here. These men will be arrested. There will be no killing."

"It is beyond that." Partlan motioned to Kimi. "They have threatened a woman, injured a fellow Hunter, and lied about their purpose. Our rules are very clear."

"So you think you can just kill people willy nilly?" Jake reached for his gun. "I'll arrest you then."

Partlan raised an eyebrow and then turned to Niail. "Does he not know?"

Niail sighed. "He knows, but he still does not understand."

"We do not answer to your laws. We live by the code that we have followed since time began."

Jake shook his head. "Mark said that you have a business of sorts, but that doesn't concern me. You're breaking the law."

Eluwilussit put a restraining hand on Jake's arm. "These are good men. You should not interfere."

"I took an oath." The gun wavered in Jake's hand. "You can't expect me to ignore that."

"They are not your enemy." Eluwilussit pointed to Partlan's arm. "They wear the symbols of the Star People and they defend. That is all you need to know."

Jake looked at his grandfather and then back at Partlan. "I don't believe that stuff."

"That is your right, but you should honor your heritage and traditions." Eluwilussit's voice was sad. "You talk as if you only care about the laws of this country. What about the sacred laws of your people?"

"Listen to Grandfather."

Kimi went to stand beside her brother. Niail moved a step closer to her and readied himself for any attack. Even though Jake was her brother and probably would not hurt her, he could not take the chance. If Jake moved on Kimi, he would kill him, brother or not.

"Don't tell me you believe this stuff?"

"These men are different." Kimi looked back at Niail. "They are no threat to us. They will not let you arrest them."

"I have to try."

"No." Kimi reached her hand up and took the gun from Jake. "You have to trust."

Niail released the breath he had been holding and took the gun from Kimi. He sensed, more than heard, a silent message going between Partlan and the others. He tried to focus and hear the conversation. A searing pain behind his eyes was his reward.

Ranon touched his arm and shook his head. "You only make it worse. It will come back in time."

Niail clenched his jaw and nodded. All he could do was wait. He had no control over his healing. He would just have to learn to accept it. He turned away from the others and went to the window. If he could not be part of the plans then what good was he?

It was a several seconds later when he heard someone approach. Partlan gripped his shoulder. "We will work around this."

"I am useless without my hearing."

"We communicate in many ways." Partlan's voice was low. "Eye and hand motions are effective."

"But not preferred."

"Listen to Ranon. He is clan Leigh. He doctors us better than anyone."

"This is new. He has not come across this before.

"No." Partlan's voice was serious. "It will not be the last time though. On this planet we are more likely to be banged up and shot than killed outright."

"I am alive." Niail's voice was wry. "I am a fool to want instant healing."

"No, you are impatient to finish the job."

"These men are dangerous." Niail sighed and turned away from the window. "Jake has underestimated their abilities."

"If they took you out, then they are some of the worse humans we have seen." Partlan grinned at Niail. "You are the toughest warrior I know."

Niail walked to the table and sat. "There is no way that only one person should go in."

"I agree." Partlan motioned for Gur, Turlo, Ranon, and Malac. "Five should be enough. I need you to stay here in case anyone else shows up."

"What about me?" Jake interjected.

"We cannot be responsible." Partlan opened the door. "We need to get this body taken care of. Do you have any suggestions?"

"We could take him and the gun back to where we left the others." Eluwilussit stood up from the chair he had been resting on. "It will look as if he died in the battle."

"What others?"

"Some of Kowal's men."

"They found us on the reservation." Niail rubbed a hand over his face. So much had happened since he had woken up. Perhaps the best thing would be for him to stay back and let the others handle Kowal.

Jake blocked the door. "Why should I trust you guys? Apparently you were hired to kill me because he was too busy to do it himself."

Partlan looked at him. "We would never kill a police officer unless he was deceitful."

"According to Mark that is what Niail said and he ended up being left for dead." Jake's voice held a note of respect. "Mark was my partner. Dishonest or not, it won't do his family any good to find out about his other activities. If Grandfather and I take him back to where the other bodies are, then no one need know about his betrayal."

Partlan held Jake's gaze for a few seconds. "You wish to protect his loved ones. That is an honorable intention. It also means you will not know what happened to Kowal."

"I hadn't thought about that, but you're right. The less I know the better."

"And the safer we'll be." Turlo chuckled. "I love how people on this planet work within the rules."

Jake opened his mouth to say something and then shut it. Niail hid his smile. As much as it had been suggested that Hunters were not from earth, Jake still had not believed it. It was just as well. The fewer people who knew, the better.

"It is settled. We will help you load the body onto your truck. Then you can leave knowing that everything will be solved when you return."

Jake and his grandfather went outside with the others.

"Do you have any weapons?" Partlan paused at the door.

Niail nodded. "They are in the back of the truck.

"Good."

Niail sensed Kimi's uncertainty. He turned to her, sending out a wave of calm. One day they might be mated. For now it was enough to know that she was his pair bond.

"I need to understand how I was captured." Niail took Kimi's hand in his. "My brothers may have answers for me."

"Anything that will help you remember." Kimi smiled and Niail's world glowed brighter.

"You should try and phone Ann. Partlan will have a phone." Niail raised her hand to his mouth and gave it a quick kiss. "We both need to know the children are fine."

Kimi nodded. She ran out after Partlan and returned with his cell phone. She flipped the phone open and walked into the bedroom. The sooner they knew about Peta and Wil, the easier both of them would feel. He exhaled and leaned back in the chair. His head still ached, but some of the fogginess was lifting. Perhaps it was being with his brothers.

Whatever it was, he just wanted his link to them to return. Once he could mind connect, then he would be able to sense Kimi's desires. According to their leader, Ardal, who already had a mate, the connection between a pair bond was intense.

He wanted to feel that connection with Kimi.

At that moment Kimi came back into the kitchen. She sighed and sat beside him. "Ann says they're both sleeping."

"That is good." Niail sat with his elbows on the table. "We know that they are safe."

The door opened and Partlan entered. He was followed by Turlo, Gur, and Malac.

"Ranon has gone with Jake and his grandfather." Partlan pulled a chair out and took the phone that Kimi held out to him. "He will join us when they have finished."

Niail cleared his throat. "Do you know how I became injured?"

Partlan looked at Gur. "Tell him."

"It's our fault. Turlo and I were on the mission with you." Gur straightened his shoulders and looked Niail in the eye. "We're still learning the ways of battle. You asked us to be ready if something wasn't right."

Kimi frowned. "I don't understand. I thought all of you had been trained since birth."

Niail reached over and squeezed her hand. "Gur and Turlo have been stranded on Earth since they were children. Their training was never completed."

"How awful." Kimi's tone was gentle. "How long have you been here?"

"We have been on your planet for over thirty years. There were many who survived the crash, but few of our number still exist." Gur straightened his shoulders. "We were not welcomed here and have had to do some questionable things to survive."

"I can imagine. Some people use fear and ignorance to justify horrible atrocities." Kimi shuddered.

"We used to believe all humans were cruel." Turlo grimaced. "We have since learned otherwise."

Niail cleared his throat. "The survivors of the crash have agreed to follow the Code that all Hunters live by. They continue their training with us. Gur and Turlo have learned much."

"We failed you." Gur's jaw tightened.

"You followed procedure." Niail's voice was firm. "You did nothing wrong."

"We weren't quick enough when they attacked."

"You once said that humans knew nothing about battle." Niail's voice was dry. "It seems you were wrong."

"Yes." Gur cleared his throat. "In the past we've done the job we were paid for. There was no need to ask questions or determine if it were a just cause. We were mercenaries for hire."

"Now you must act with honor." Partlan crossed his arms. "That means being prepared when others have none."

"And we weren't prepared." Gur looked past Niail's shoulder. "Because of our inexperience you were captured."

Niail leaned back in his chair. He did not remember what had happened with Kowal's men, but he was certain that it was not Gur and Turlo's fault. They were both good warriors. They had been abandoned on a hostile planet and survived. They had skills, which might be different from his, but still useful.

"You are my brothers." Niail's voice was low. "There is no blame."

Gur's shoulders relaxed. "The meeting was held in an empty warehouse. You told us to take a position on the second floor. We had our rifles aimed, but they were useless once they surrounded you."

"How did they capture me?"

Gur shrugged. "We couldn't hear the conversation from where we were, but at some point you looked to be arguing."

"That was probably when Kowal was telling me he wanted Jake killed."

"You refused." Partlan rubbed his nose. "You communicated that much to me."

"Then they stabbed you with a syringe. You fought, but you were stumbling and striking out at the air. Whatever they gave you, it weakened and incapacitated you almost instantly."

"Why didn't you shoot the men?"

"One of them held you from behind." Gur's tone was apologetic. "My rifle jammed, so I threw it down and went to attack, but you told me to stay clear."

Niail frowned. "I must have thought I could handle it."

"You did not want Gur and Turlo captured." Partlan's voice rang out clear. "You relayed that it was an ambush. That was the last word I heard from you."

"So I was trying to protect them."

"It would appear that way." Partlan leaned on the table. "You were explicit in your directions to them. You wanted them to retreat."

"Maybe Kowal was threatening something big, like an explosion." Kimi's voice was hesitant. "Mark said that he was prepared for the possibility that you would find out that he had lied in his request. He must have had a back-up plan."

Niail searched his brain, but all he got was a blank. It made sense that Kowal would be prepared if they refused his business. The man had survived as a criminal for years. That would only have happened with advanced planning capabilities.

"You believe he told me what he threatened, and I made the others abandon the site?"

Partlan nodded. "That sounds like you Niail. If it were a trap you would have wanted the others to leave."

"Our training has been different. In the past we would have rushed in and rescued you." Gur's voice held confusion. "Protecting each other from humans was our first priority."

"Niail would not have expected that." Partlan shook his head. "The honorable thing would have been to save his brothers, especially if the odds were not in favor of a victory."

"It is what any of us would do." Malac's voice was firm. "When there is no chance of survival, we retreat. That allows us to come at it from a different direction."

Gur swallowed. "But we didn't obey."

Niail grinned. "That does not surprise me. What did you do?"

"We followed them. When they reached a deserted road they threw you off a truck. Their guns were aimed at you so Turlo and I created a diversion."

"You were the reason they left in a hurry." Niail's voice held admiration. "You saved my life."

"We circled around to come back for you, but you were gone."

"Bobby." Kimi shook her head. "He saw the men drive off and he took Niail away before they could return."

"So both Bobby and you saved my life." A surge of gratitude went through him. Their actions had led him to Kimi. "You showed yourself to be warriors of honor. Thank you."

"We disobeyed."

Partlan pushed back from the table. "You obeyed the order to retreat. Planning a rescue was the actions of a true warrior. You are learning."

"Niail was still lost."

"I was saved." Niail stood. "In more ways than you could possibly understand."

"Now we must deal with Kowal." Partlan walked to the door. "We must destroy him."

Niail hesitated a second before speaking. "I am the one that was dishonored. I should finish the job."

"True, but you are not healed."

"I am still a warrior." Niail kept his voice low. "My help would be of use."

"I will not risk your life on such a simple mission."

The death of Kowal should be at his hands. Injured or not, he was capable of demanding satisfaction. The others had opened the door to leave. Niail had to warn them. Kowal would be ready for them."

"It will not be easy. He has sent several men to kill me."

"That is all the more reason for us to defeat him without you." Partlan crossed his arms. "He knows you. We will be a surprise."

"True, but I understand how he thinks."

Niail looked back at Kimi. Her eyes were filled with fear. He sent her a surge of reassurance and hoped she would understand. He had to make certain that Kowal did not live. That was the only way she would be safe.

Partlan paused. He frowned and then shook his head. "You cannot remember what happened. You need to heal."

"I am still a Hunter."

"And as such, you will follow your orders." Partlan's voice was decisive. "You are to wait at the rendezvous site.

Ardal has already been made aware of the situation. Once we deal with Kowal, we will depart this area."

"I cannot leave Kimi."

Partlan looked at her and nodded. "She still needs protection. I will have Ranon stay here once he returns with her brother and Eluwilussit. When the mission is finished he can join us."

"You do not understand." Niail's tone was sharp. "I have bonded with Kimi. I will not leave her when she is in danger."

Chapter 18

Silence followed Niail's words. Kimi held her breath and waited for their reaction. Partlan's hand dropped to his side and the others came to a full stop. It was obvious Niail's announcement had shocked them.

"This is true?" Malac's tone sounded awed. "We were beginning to believe that only Ardal would find a mate."

"She is my pair bond. I have no doubts." Niail cleared his throat and walked toward her. "We are not mated."

"But you are bonded." Partlan straightened his shoulders. "That makes it imperative that she is protected."

"There is more." Niail rubbed at his temple. "Kimi has two children, Peta, and Wil. I have vowed to protect them also."

"They are safe now?" Partlan's voice was clipped.

"Yes. Kimi just checked on them."

"There is only one course of action." Partlan crossed his arms over his chest. "You need to stay with your pair bond. We have all vowed to protect the mates of our brothers, but I understand the need is greater when it is your own pair bond."

"There is only way to do that. Kowal must be defeated." Niail took her hand in his. "Death is the only certainty that she and her children will be safe."

"He has lied to us, tried to kill us, and now he threatens women and children. He is a man without honor. He cannot continue to live."

Kimi shuddered as a shiver of ice raced up her spine. She didn't believe in killing. It went against everything she held sacred. There was no denying what Partlan had said though. Kowal wouldn't stop until Niail was dead.

Her heart skipped a beat. The threat to Niail was

personal. To think of him not being with her, forced the air from her lungs. She couldn't bear to lose him. Not now. Not after just finding him.

It hit her with blinding clarity.

She was in love with Niail.

Illogical as it was, she loved him whole heartedly, and irrevocably. What had started out as an electrifying attraction had developed until she couldn't bear the thought of life without him. She could no longer hide or deny how she felt.

It was crazy. He wasn't Blackfeet. He wasn't even Native American. He didn't understand their traditions, or how important it was for her children to learn the ways of her people. She had struggled and sacrificed to ensure that they wouldn't be caught between two worlds like Jake. She wanted them to be proud of their heritage.

Somehow Niail sensed her confusion because he squeezed her hand. "I know this is difficult, but I must protect you."

"Is there no other way?" Kimi's chest tightened at the thought of more people dying. "Perhaps Jake will be successful in getting him arrested?"

Niail shook his head. "The man has broken our code. I think he has broken many of your traditions also."

"True." Kimi inhaled a shaky breath. "He is also endangering our youth. I just believe that people should be given a chance to change."

"He has shown himself to be evil." Partlan's tone brooked no argument. "This is what we have been bred and trained for."

"There would be no real safety for you or the children if he lived." Niail leaned close. "I could never rest knowing he might do you harm."

"Could you let Jake go with you?" Kimi looked at Partlan. "He should be able to get some police to help you."

"The law enforcement on this planet does not approve of our methods."

"They might use us, but they consider us beneath humans." Gur spoke in a sharp tone. "They send us in to do what they don't have the stomach for."

Kimi's eyes widened. She looked over at Niail and then back to Partlan. "The police know about you?"

"Not the police, but the government."

She closed her eyes for a second. It shouldn't surprise her. Monitoring technology was so advanced that some hidden government agency probably knew where everyone was at any given time. It was inconceivable that alien warriors could be on the planet without some secret agency knowing of their existence.

"If the government knows about you, then they must support your actions."

"They cannot find us." Partlan took a step closer to her. "We stay hidden from them. Since our crash landing on your planet eight months ago, no Hunter will work for the government. They have not been generous to us in the past."

"So you live a life on the run?"

"Yes." Niail answered her. "It is safer. It is also the best way for us to protect others."

Kimi nodded. It made sense in a strange way. If the traditions of her people were correct, then these men were from the stars. They would never be safe on this planet. With a shiver she realized what it would mean to love a Hunter. She would have to choose between Niail and her traditions.

"It does not need to be so." Niail leaned close to her. "There are ways to deal with this."

"You will always be moving around."

Niail shook his head. "I will always be where you are."

Partlan cleared his throat. "We must leave. Niail, you will stay with your pair bond. We will deal with Kowal. When

Jake returns, you can let him know where to find us. We should be finished by the time he reaches us."

"It is best." Niail stood. "I need to be near Kimi to sense if she is in danger."

"Until you are healed, there is no other solution." Partlan opened the door and the others left the house. "Your new orders are to make certain she is safe."

"Understood." Niail moved to the door. "I will stay here until you have finished the operation."

"We will come for you." Partlan stood in the doorway. "If you are still unable to mind connect we will work out a solution. We will leave you here until you are ready to join us."

Niail nodded. "As you command."

"I will let the others know what has happened."

"By Cygnus and Warrior, we will win."

Kimi sighed when the door closed behind Partlan. Niail turned and looked at her for a second and then went to the stove to turn the kettle on. He opened and shut a couple of cupboards before he found the one with the mugs. He pulled out two. He put scoops of hot chocolate in each cup and left them near the stove, before turning back to her.

Kimi pushed a strand of hair behind her ear with shaky fingers. "I can't believe we're safe?"

"You are overwhelmed."

"Yes." Kimi's shoulders sagged. "I'm also tired, frightened, in shock, and totally confused."

"It is over." Niail poured hot water into the mugs. "You can relax. Partlan and the others will deal with Kowal."

Suddenly it was all too much. She trembled with reaction. She started to rub her arms as cold shivers racked her body. The past two days had been a nightmare. If Niail hadn't been by her side, she never would have survived it. He had been her anchor.

Niail put the mugs of hot chocolate on the table, before sitting next to her. He pulled his chair close and gathered her into his arms. A sense of calm enveloped her.

"Put it out of your mind." Niail pushed the hot drink toward her.

"I'll never forget the horror of it." Tears started fill her eyes. "Every time I heard a gunshot I thought you were dead."

Niail's fingers brushed the hair from her face. His touch sent quivers of warmth throughout her body. "I am careful."

Kimi let out a shaky breath. "Look at your injuries. None of these would have happened if I hadn't insisted you stay with me."

"Then I would not have been given the privilege of protecting you." Niail feathered a kiss on her forehead.

"I've been nothing but trouble." Kimi moaned. "I was never more terrified than when you came back to the truck with your head sliced open."

"It was not serious."

"The last thing you needed was another head wound." Kimi looked up at him and blinked back her tears. "You've suffered so much to keep us alive."

"I would do even more."

"I don't want you getting hurt again." Kimi shivered as the vision of him lying on the ground, bleeding and injured burrowed into her brain. "It would be too much for me to endure."

"I will always return to you."

Kimi gazed up at him and her heart melted. Truth and devotion shone from the depths of Niail's dark eyes. He accepted her unconditionally. He protected those who couldn't defend themselves. It was an honorable vocation. She knew she loved him, but could she risk living with the upheaval he would bring to her existence.

What was the alternative?

A life without Niail? Every cell in her body rebelled against the thought. He filled her being. She didn't exist when he was away from her. When he was near, it was all she could do to keep from touching him. His presence gave her peace.

Kimi lowered her head to his chest. "I don't deserve you."

"You are the gift." Niail's voice was low. "Never did I dream that I would find my pair bond. Just being with you, holding you close, gives my life purpose."

"Your work is dangerous. What if something happens to you?" Kimi's voice faltered. "If I let you into my life, I'll never be the same."

"I will be happy with whatever you decide." Niail's hand brushed down her back, soothing in its touch. "I will never leave you. I am content to stand guard and keep you safe for the rest of my life."

It was crazy, but she believed him. He was not the same as human men. He lived by a code of honor that was reminiscent of her people when they still roamed the plains.

He would stay by her side always.

"Even if you do not desire me," Niail whispered. "I will not mate with another woman."

"Ever?" Kimi's eyes widened and she lifted her head from his chest. "What if I chose another?"

"Then I will accept that, but the pair bond will not be broken unless you desire that."

"That means you will know my thoughts and worries."

"I will be able to keep you safe."

Kimi looked down at the table. Niail's words seemed insane. No human man would agree to such an existence.

Still, he had endured worse in his life. Suddenly, she knew that the one thing she wanted more than anything was to give him joy.

She loved him.

If her heart was trampled on again, then she would deal with that later. She glanced up at Niail. A flame of desire danced within his eyes. A shiver of awareness skittered across her body. This man was worth risking her heart on.

She leaned closer. His breath skimmed across her cheek. Her mouth went dry. It was intoxicating to be this close. She inhaled a shaky breath. She was ready to take the next step.

"I want to make love with you.

"You wish to be my mate?" Niail's voice held hope.

"It's too soon for me to know." Kimi smoothed her fingers over his chest. "I do know I love you. The best way I know how to express that is physically. After everything we've been through I need to hold you. I want to know that what we share is real."

Niail reached for her hand. "You must guide me. Men from my planet exist only to give satisfaction to the women. I wish to do the same for you."

"I've only ever been with my ex-husband." Kimi tried to keep the nervousness out of her voice. "This will be like the first time for me too."

Niail pulled her off the chair and into his arms. His lips skimmed over hers sending a shock through her body. "I am impatient to pleasure you. Since the first moment I opened my eyes, I knew there was something between us.

"You were too sick to think about anything." Kimi nipped at his chin.

"Your eyes called to me." Niail's tongue slid across the seal of her lips. "Your voice brought me back to life."

Niail captured her mouth and a searing rush of need

raced through her veins. She opened for him, savoring the delectable trill of excitement that shot through her when his tongue curled about hers.

The world spun, and she was lost in his touch. His arms held her secure and she let her hands roam around his neck and shoulders. He was solid and safe. A sense of belonging and love surrounded her. Nothing in her life had ever felt so right.

Niail scooped her into his arms. He cradled her legs and body close to his chest and walked to the bedroom. Her fingers reached into his dark hair and teased a groan from him. He didn't stop moving. It wasn't until they had reached the bed and Niail was lowering her, that he broke the kiss.

He stood back and looked down at her. His eyes burned with passion. Her breath caught in her throat. No man had ever looked at her with such yearning. Her body surged with heat and need.

"You have too many clothes on." She hardly recognized her husky voice.

"So do you." Niail leaned down and unbuttoned her blouse. "I have longed to see you."

"The feeling is mutual." Kimi grabbed the bottom of his tee-shirt and lifted it over his head.

He was magnificent.

The bruises on his body had healed since the previous day, and except for the bandage on his side from the bullet wound, he looked unmarked. It was a miracle that he mended so quickly, but everything about this man was amazing.

The fact that he desired her was incredible.

She shrugged her blouse off. His hands hovered over her silk bra. Instead of removing it, he moved down to her jeans and unzipped them. She raised her hips and let him peal the material off.

She reached for his pants and undid the button at the waistband. He grabbed her hands and held them away from him.

"I need to enjoy you first." His voice was hoarse.

"I can't wait long."

Niail grinned. "I will remember."

He knelt on the bed. She scooted over to make room for him. He stretched out beside her and his fingers feathered across her neck and then down to her breasts.

"How do you remove this?"

Kimi guided his fingers to the front clip of her bra. He fumbled at the clasp for a second and then it opened. Cool air brushed against her heated skin to be quickly replaced by the touch of Niail's mouth.

His lips caressed and nibbled their way from her neck to her chest. He traced a path around the one breast, moving in a circular motion closer and closer to the nipple. Tension built. She moaned as a ripple of exquisite pleasure touched her inner core.

His tongue darted out and flicked the tip of her nipple. A jolt of piercing delight curled within her. Her back arched off the bed, but his hand soothed her. He left that breast and began the same journey with the other. Her breathing was ragged when he had finished.

His lips moved to her stomach. She was barely aware when his fingers skimmed her panties off her hips. His hands glided down her side as his mouth moved to her inner core. Kimi tried to stop him, but he pushed her protests aside.

His tongue licked and suckled until she was on the screaming edge of climax. Only then did Niail relent and let his lips graze her inner thighs, roaming down her legs and then back to the juncture at her hips to tease and stimulate again.

The tension built until she was on the verge of

shattering. Niail held her safe as she splintered with spasms of ecstasy.

He moved up the bed and gathered her in his arms. She floated back to earth to find him nuzzling her neck. Never had she experienced such a dizzying release. Her body still shook from the aftermath of it.

"Did I please you?"

"Any better and I would be dead." Kimi sighed and turned to face Niail. "Now it's my turn."

Niail frowned. "You are ready again?"

"More than ready." She pushed Niail onto his back and got up on her knees. She reached for the waistband of his jeans. "I get to enjoy you."

She pulled his jeans off with one smooth yank. She disposed of his underwear in the same fashion. She sat back on her feet and let her eyes devour him.

Every inch of him was firm and large.

Her hand slid down his chest. She hesitated before moving lower, letting a finger glide down the long length of his manhood. A shiver of desire jolted through and settled within her womb. She took a shaky breath. She would savor every moment of loving this man.

She eased up the bed and nibbled at his lips. He gathered her close in his arms. She slid her tongue against his, laving and rubbing until her body tingled and sizzled. She left his mouth and let her lips roam lower. She nipped his chin and rubbed her cheek against the stubble there. She sighed as the friction sent a shiver of pleasure through her.

Loving Niail was all that existed.

She could become addicted to the feel of him beneath her hands. She sat back and kneaded his chest, letting her fingers circle his nipples and then pinch them. A jolt rippled through his body and he groaned.

She was enthralled.

There was nothing she wouldn't do to bring this man pleasure. Her lips followed her fingers. She caressed and nipped his firm chest, feathering her tongue across his scars and bruises. The world faded, leaving only the taste and feel of Niail.

Her lips moved down his chest and lingered on his firm abdomen. Her tongue swirled and licked until her body was weeping with moist heat. Loving Niail was exciting her to a fever pitch.

Her tongue slid down the long length of Niail's manhood. He jumped and tried to push her away, but she held firm. She tasted him before taking him into her mouth. His body shook and tensed with her ministrations.

She wanted more.

She needed to feel him inside of her.

Releasing him, she sat up and then straddled his hips. With shaking fingers she guided him. He held her hips, his eyes never leaving hers as she eased herself down onto him. She shivered with the thrill of him stretching her completely. Then he thrust up into her and she was lost.

Niail plunged deep.

It was exquisite.

He withdrew and repeated the movement. Kimi matched his rhythm until the only thing that existed was the spiral of ecstasy that was building within them. Their gazes were locked as they strove to reach the pinnacle together, plummeting over the edge in a rapture that left Kimi's whole body throbbing with bliss.

She collapsed onto Niail. His arms pulled her close. She shuddered at the enormity of what had happened between them. She started to shiver and Niail threw a cover over them. Tears filled her eyes and trickled down her cheek. The truth was now clear to her.

She couldn't live without Niail.

It didn't matter that he wasn't Blackfeet, or that he wasn't human. The only thing that mattered was that she needed to be with him always.

"Sleep." Niail's voice was a whisper, his breath a soft caress against her cheeks. "I will be here when you awake."

Kimi looked up. Her eyes scanned his beloved face and then met his gaze. "I love you."

"You are the only woman I will ever desire." Niail kissed her forehead. "There could never be another."

"I need to feel you close."

"Our bond strengthens." Niail's fingers framed her face. "That is how I know you need to rest."

Kimi yawned and then dropped her head onto his chest. He was right. They had been traveling non-stop all day and that didn't include the emotional upheaval of fighting for their lives. A few minutes in his arms and she knew that the world would right itself.

She didn't know how long she slept, but she knew what woke her. It was the pounding on her door and Ann's voice yelling.

"Kimi, you need to open the door. Wil and Peta have been kidnapped."

Niail jumped from the bed and pulled on his jeans and tee-shirt. Kimi was slower to move. Ann's words echoed through her head. She couldn't make sense of them. Why would anyone want to hurt the children?

She had just sat up when Niail handed her clothes over. Her hands shook so he laid them on the bed. She pulled on her pants, but her fingers fumbled over the buttons of her blouse.

"What if something happens to them?" Her voice trembled.

"I will protect them. I will do whatever it takes."

Niail buttoned the blouse and then helped her stand.

He kept his arm around her shoulders and led her out of the room. When she was safe in a kitchen chair he went to the door.

Kimi struggled for breath. Her brain refused to grasp what Ann had said. She couldn't make sense of Ann's words. Everything seemed to be happening outside her body as she watched Niail unlocked the door. Ann pushed past him and stopped beside Kimi.

"Men came to my house and took the kids." Her voice was breathless. She pulled out a chair and sat. "We have to call the police."

"No." Niail closed the door. "Did they say what they wanted?"

Ann shook her head. "It made no sense."

"Tell me."

"They barged into the house and went straight to where the kids were sleeping." Ann's voice shook.

The words swirled in Kimi's head. Her pulse sped and every muscle in her body tensed as a surge of anger boiled inside of her. Her children were gone. Her babies were in the hands of monsters.

"Stop." Her voice shook as she looked at Ann. "How could you let them take them?"

"I tried to prevent them, but they were too big for me."

"I trusted you with them." Kimi grabbed Ann's arm and shook it. "It was the only thing I asked. Keep the children safe."

"There were five of them and they had guns. Two held me back while the others grabbed the kids from their beds." Ann started to sob. "I'm sorry Kimi. I wish they had taken me instead."

Niail crouched down beside her. "Ann is not to blame. I am."

Kimi shook her head. What was he saying? "You were here."

"I failed to protect them." Niail eased her hand off Ann's arm. "Your friend has bruises and cuts to her face and arms. She fought to keep the children safe."

Kimi frowned. For the first time she looked at Ann's appearance. Her blouse was ripped at one arm and the collar was torn off. Her right cheek had a large red mark across it and her lip was bleeding. She inhaled a deep breath and forced back her anger and pain.

Kimi touched Ann's arm. "I know you did everything you could."

"It just didn't make sense what they wanted." Ann pulled a tissue from her pant pocket. "They said I had to bring them the hunter."

The horror of what had happened settled like lead in her stomach. Kowal's men had taken the children.

Chapter 19

Kimi gasped. She shook her head and turned to look at Niail. A wave of despair hit him so hard that he almost took a step back. Her feelings were his.

Niail pushed all emotion away. He needed a clear head if he was going to save the children. And save them he would. There was nothing he would not do for Kimi. Death would be a small price to pay to keep her and the children safe.

His heart pounded hard against his chest. A surge of adrenaline raced through his body as everything in him prepared for battle. His breeding and training took over. He was all Hunter.

He reached over and squeezed her shoulder. "I will gladly give them what they want."

Kimi's voice was choked with tears. "They'll kill you."

"They will try." Niail took her hands in his. "I promised to keep you safe and I will."

"By sacrificing yourself?" Kimi choked back a sob. "That's not what I want."

"It is necessary." Niail bent and kissed her hands.

"I don't understand. What's going on here?" Ann's voice was full of confusion. "Who is the hunter?"

"I am a Hunter." Niail stood up. "It is me they want."

"How do you know?" Ann frowned. "Most men in this area hunt."

"He's not that kind of hunter." Kimi sighed. "It was Kowal's men who took Wil and Peta. They know that I've been taking care of Niail."

"You mean the guy who owns the furniture store?" Ann rubbed the side of her head. "Why would he want a hunter so desperately that he would kidnap two children?"

"He knows I will exchange myself for them."

Niail went to one of the sideboard drawers and opened it. He pulled out two handguns from the stash he had left earlier. He popped out the cartridges in both, checked the number of bullets. He put one of the guns into back of his jean's waistband. He kept the other gun in his hand.

"It is what a Hunter would do." He went to the door.

"That's the first time I've heard that about hunters." Ann stood and helped Kimi to her feet. "Usually they only stick around long enough to butcher and divide the meat."

Niail reached for Kimi's hand. Her silence worried him. Her fingers were cold and he rubbed them to give her some warmth. Her eyes stayed blank and she did not turn to him.

"I am a warrior."

Ann took a deep breath. "I still think we should call the police."

"That would be dangerous."

"Not any riskier than you trading yourself for the kids." Ann pulled her keys from her pocket. "We can take my car."

"Good." Niail closed the door to the house. "Kimi's truck is not here."

"Where are we to meet them?" Kimi's voice trembled.

"He wants to meet on the old Browning road, outside of town." Ann unlocked the rear door.

"He's going to do the exchange on the reservation?" Kimi's hand shook as she reached for the handle. "That's awfully bold of him."

"Or smart." Niail held the door while Kimi got in. "He probably thinks the police are now aware of his activities and are watching his warehouse."

Ann went to slide behind the driver's seat, but Niail held his hands out for the keys. "It is safer if I drive there."

"It's my car." Ann's voice was defensive.

"Kimi needs your support." Niail put the extra gun on the seat beside him. "Give me the directions and I will get us there."

"Men," Ann muttered under her breath as she walked around to the front passenger seat. "Always think they're the only ones who can handle anything."

Kimi touched Ann's arm when she slid into the car. "Niail will keep us safe."

"The police are needed. We can't go out there half-cocked with weapons. Someone could get hurt."

"People are already dead." Kimi's voice was low. "I don't want Wil or Peta hurt. Niail will do what is necessary."

Ann glanced over at him. "How do you know? I thought he was dragged into your place half dead."

"We have been running from Kowal's men since I left the kids at your house."

Niail started the engine. "I need to finish this business with Kowal. It is the only way Kimi and the children will ever be safe."

"I don't like the sound of this." Ann's hand was on the door handle. "Maybe I should get out now?"

"That's up to you Ann." Kimi sighed. "It might be safer if you stayed here."

"You're scaring me." Ann's voice held a hint of horror. "What aren't you telling me?"

"Kowal will try to kill me." Niail's hand rested on the steering wheel. "That is why I must get the children to you before I exchange myself. It will give you a chance to escape."

"That's absurd."

Ann's words fell on silence. She looked back at Kimi and then over at Niail. In the faint light from the car's dashboard Niail could make out the horror on her face.

"Say something," Ann begged.

"Niail is speaking the truth." Kimi wiped a hand over her face. "Our lives are in danger. It might be best for you to stay out of it."

"He's already been to my house." Ann's voice had dropped to a whisper. "That means I'm not safe either."

Niail put the car in drive. "I will do my best to keep you protected."

"How?" Ann twisted around to face Kimi. "Does Jake know about this?"

"Yes, but he is with Grandfather right now. He won't be able to help." Kimi's voice sounded faint from the rear. "What are your plans Niail?"

"I will get Wil and Peta to you before I hand myself over to Kowal." He gave the spare gun back to Kimi. "Use this to protect yourselves. As soon as the kids are in the car you drive as fast as you can to the police."

"I'll drive." Ann's voice boomed with decisiveness. "The kids will be upset. They'll need you Kimi."

"What about you Niail?"

"I will stay and kill Kowal."

"And his men will shoot you." Kimi's voice shook with unshed tears.

"They will try, but many of them will be slain first."

Ann cleared her throat. "Are we talking a massacre here?"

"This is about justice." Niail clenched his jaw.

Kimi leaned forward, her hand touching his shoulder. A shiver of awareness chased through him. To have known paradise and then lose it was too painful to think about. He forced his thoughts back to the children. He would do everything in his power to stay alive, but if necessary he would die protecting his pair bond.

"What about the others?"

"I cannot connect with them." Niail silently cursed his injury. "I will stand alone."

They drove in silence for several miles. The darkness of the evening was absolute. There were no street lights to illuminate their way. The low cloud cover only added to the suffocating feel of the night. The only light was from the headlights of the car as they drove toward their destination.

"There it is." Ann's hand pointed to the right.

Niail looked over. There was a clearing with an unearthly glow hovering over it. It looked as if the beams of several vehicles were illuminating an area. The light was bouncing off the clouds and creating a bigger circle of brightness. This was where he would make a stand against Kowal.

The man deserved death.

Honor demanded satisfaction.

The only question was whether Niail would be able to survive the fight. He knew with a certainty that he would be able to live long enough to kill most of the men responsible for the kidnapping. He was not certain if he could kill them all.

That meant that he would have to rely on his brother Hunters to do the deed once he was dead. In order to do this, Kimi had to escape with the children and contact Partlan. There was no other way.

He slowed the vehicle down and leaned forward. His eyes scanned the road until he saw a dirt path off to the right. He turned and brought the car to a stop. He twisted around and looked at Kimi.

"Once you have the children, I want you to drive away as fast as possible. Do not stop."

"You can't expect me to leave you there alone?" Kimi's shook her head.

Niail turned to Ann. "Promise that you will drive away and not come back."

Ann looked back at Kimi and then nodded. "If that's what you want."

"It is."

"What about you?" Kimi grabbed his shoulder. "I can't leave you there."

"You need to contact Partlan." Niail winced as the full force of Kimi's distress filled him. "They will protect you."

"I don't want protection." Kimi's words were a sob. "I want the children and you."

Niail put the car into gear and started down the path. He wanted her more than anything in the whole world, but he was a warrior first. He knew his duty. Right now all he could focus on was getting Wil and Peta back into their mother's arms. After that, he would do the best he could to stay alive.

They reached a circle of vehicles a couple of minutes down the path. Niail stopped the car several yards away. There were no lights behind them. Kimi would have an escape route.

"You should be able to swing the car around here without interference. Scoot over to the driver's side as soon as I leave the vehicle. You may not have enough time later."

Ann cleared her throat. "We're really going to do this?"

Niail looked over at her. "It is necessary."

"What if something happens?"

"These are not men of honor." Niail's voice was devoid of emotion. "They will lie. They will try and stop you. Do not let them."

"How are we going to prevent that?" Ann waved her hands at the headlights glaring at them. "There are too many of them. Is it even worth trying to fight?"

"Never surrender." Niail clasped Ann's hand in his. "You are the driver. That means everything depends on you. Can you do this?"

Ann bit her lip. "I don't know."

"The children will need comforting." Niail looked back at Kimi. "Will you be able to drive?"

Kimi took a shaky breath. "Yes."

Niail sensed her strength and determination. Kimi was focused on saving her children now. Gone was her anger and shock. In its place was cold resolve. He knew she would do what was necessary to get the children to safety.

"Trade places."

Niail watched as Ann climbed into the back and Kimi came forward. He needed someone with fortitude to push through what was to come. Kowal would not let them drive away. He would stop them from escaping because they were witnesses. Niail would do his best to kill all of the men, but Kimi must escape.

He looked back at Ann. "When the children are in the car, make certain they lay down on the floor. If necessary you must cover them with your body. I do not want them to see what I must do."

Ann rubbed her arms. "Okay."

"Promise." Niail's voice was insistent. "It is very important."

"I understand." Ann's tone was stronger. "I don't want to see what's going to happen, so I will definitely cover them."

Niail nodded. "Good." He turned to Kimi. "You must drive, no matter what."

"What are you expecting?"

"Kowal will try to stop you." Niail reached out and touched her cheek. "I will prevent that, but you have to drive away. No matter what you hear or see."

Kimi choked back a sob. "Come back to me."

"It is all I think about." Niail's voice was low. "You are the only thing that matters."

Niail twisted in his seat. She reached for him and lifted her face. His lips clung to hers. Passion and desire raged within him, but he put it aside to send her reassurance, and love. He surrounded her with peace.

"I must go." Niail left the car running and opened the door. "Use the gun to protect yourselves."

He stepped out of the car.

A voice shouted out of the darkness. "You're a hard man to kill."

Niail straightened his shoulders. The cold metal of the gun in his waistband gave him comfort. He would be able to get at least one shot off before they got him. For a second he wished he had a disintegrator, but that was not to be. He was on earth now, and must fight with the weapons this planet provided.

"Where are the children?" Niail's voice slashed the air. "I will not move until I see them."

He heard a car door open and then the scramble of feet. Into the blinding headlights of one of the vehicles he saw Wil and Peta pushed forward. A surge of anger raced through him. How dare they mistreat children? Every sacred tenet that he lived by was being broken tonight.

Niail took a deep calming breath. Anger would not save Kimi and the children. Determination replaced the anger. Hunter blood flowed through his veins. Never had anything mattered so much to him. His pair bond and her children were in danger.

He would not fail.

If necessary, he would die for them.

He took one step forward. "Send the children."

Niail's training took over. He might be alone, but he was the best marksmen in the unit. He would succeed.

"Go." A voice boomed from beyond the headlights.

Peta was in the lead. She held Wil's hand and led the two of them into the center of the circle of light. Her lower lip quivered. Her eyes darted back and forth, but she kept walking. Wil held a blanket close to his chest, his head half buried in it.

"I am here, Peta." Niail kept his voice gentle. "Keep walking. Soon you will be with your mother."

Wil's head shot up. "Is that you Niail?"

"It is." Niail took another step forward. "You just have a few more steps."

"Now you start walking." The same gruff voice from beyond the headlights barked. "I want to make sure you're the right guy."

Niail took another two steps. "A Hunter never lies. As soon as the children are safe, then I will come with you."

"You guys never give up, either." The voice started laughing. "You thought you would get the best of me, but I fooled you. I'll do anything to get what I want."

"You should never have contacted aHunter4Hire." Niail could not keep the sneer out of his voice. "Our contract is very specific. We do not allow our honor to be besmirched."

"You can talk all you want about honor, but I have you now."

Niail's took another step forward. The children were a few feet away. They had to continue on to the car no matter what happened next. When they were even with him, he crouched down beside them.

"I need you both to be very brave." Niail touched Peta's cheek. "Remember, you have the spirit of a warrior."

Peta nodded. A slight tremor of the hand that clung to her brother was all that Niail noticed. Beside her, Wil was looking at him with wide eyes. His blanket covered his mouth, but his eyes showed his fear.

Niail swallowed. "I am going over to those men now. You have to keep walking to the car behind me."

"What about you?" Wil's voice was a low whine.

"I have work to do." Niail grinned. "When I am finished I will see you both."

"You mean you have to do superhero stuff." Wil nodded. "Be careful. Those men have bad medicine."

"I will remember that." Niail stood. "Now go to the car. Your mother is waiting."

Peta led her brother away. Niail's chest constricted as he thought about the children and their obvious fear. There was nothing he could do to reassure them. Instead, he focused on what he needed to do.

Kill Kowal.

He moved his neck from side to side and eased his breathing. Each step forward was one closer to his goal. His honor, and the honor of all Hunters, was at stake. He would not fail.

"Don't move any closer."

Niail stopped.

"I want to see your hands in the air." The gruff voice again. "I'm not a fool."

Niail shrugged. He put his hands in the air and waited. He was fast. Faster than any human and no matter how many bullets they might fill him with, he knew where the voice was coming from. His aim would be true. He might not survive their firepower, but Kowal would be dead also.

A man holding an assault rifle came out of the darkness. He walked toward Niail. His weapon never wavered from Niail. Behind him, Niail heard Ann's vehicle spin around, and speed off. Relief and resolve filled him. They were safe. Now he must finish this job.

Once the man was within a few feet of him he stopped. His rifle poked him in the stomach. "Move."

That's when Niail heard Ann's car screech to a stop. He looked behind and saw more headlights. They completed a ring of light. Ann's vehicle was being forced to stay within the circle. They were blocking Kimi and the children's escape.

There was no time.

He had to act now.

Niail dropped his right hand and grabbed the rifle. He lifted the weapon into the air and pulled the gunman against him at the same time. He hauled his opponent into a neck hold. Shots rang out, but Niail ignored them. He kept the man tight to him as he lowered the firearm and turned it on the headlights shining at them. He kept pressure on his captive's trigger finger and held the gun steady as it fired.

The automatic rifle made short work of the lights. That leveled the field for Niail. His vision was better on this planet. He took aim and started shooting at the men who were now scurrying to hide behind the vehicles. One by one, they dropped.

As they ran for cover, Kowal's men returned fire. Niail's captive bore the brunt of their bullets. The man's body sagged against him and his hand released the rifle. Niail dropped to the ground and used the dead man's body as a barricade. He leaned the gun against it and started shooting.

From behind him, he could hear cars racing toward him, but he did not stop firing. Kimi and the children's lives depended on his accuracy. Never before had it mattered so much.

A bullet hit the dirt beside him.

It had come from behind.

Niail flipped over onto his back and raised the rifle. He pulled the trigger and nothing happened. It was out of ammunition. He threw it away and reached for his pistol. He sat to take aim, just as the gun was kicked out of his hand.

Before he could stand four men held him down.

He was captured.

Chapter 20

Relief and anguish pounded through Kimi's veins when Wil and Peta jumped into the backseat. Their eyes were round with fear. She grabbed them close and kissed both of them. They were safe, but there was no time to waste.

The car was thrown into reverse.

She stomped on the gas pedal.

Kimi spun the car around and started driving away the second the rear door shut. What was left of her heart was pounding in her ears as she raced away from Kowal's ambush. She held back her sobs and kept praying that Niail would be able to get through this alive.

She wasn't a fool. There was no way one man could take on the number that those headlights represented. It wasn't possible, unless a miracle happened.

"Is Niail going to come?" Peta's voice was small and scared. "Shouldn't we wait for him?"

"He will meet us later." Kimi glanced over her seat. "He wants you to get on the floor. Ann will make sure you're covered up."

Just then headlights blinded her through the front windshield. For a second her mind refused to believe what she was seeing. Her heart raced. There had been nothing here when they'd driven into the clearing. Where had these vehicles come from? Her chest tightened and she had to stop herself from screaming. There was only one explanation.

They had been led into a trap.

"Keep the children down, Ann."

Kimi tightened her hold on the steering wheel. She wasn't going to let Niail's sacrifice be wasted. She would get them out of this. She steered and maneuvered around the vehicles coming at her. When she skirted around one, another blocked her exit. No matter how she twisted and directed the car, she couldn't escape. There didn't seem to be any way through them. Kowal had thought out his strategy well.

A vehicle raced directly at her. Visions of playing chicken flashed through Kimi's mind, but she couldn't risk it with the children in the back. The oncoming truck swung sideways in front of them.

She had no choice but to stop.

That's when she heard the gunfire.

Shots were firing in a rapid succession behind her. She winced as each blast was met with a scream. Her body shook. What if that was Niail getting hit. She fought the urge to go back and get him. Instead she banged her hands against the steering wheel. She had to get the children to safety.

"This is what he wanted you to do." Ann's voice was a quiet reminder. She pointed to Kimi's left. "Is there any way to go through those cars?"

Kimi steadied her breathing. She couldn't afford to panic. Too much was at risk. She inhaled and pointed the car at a space between two of the vehicles. She would just skim past the front end of the truck in front of her.

She slammed one foot on the brake and the other on the gas pedal. The engine revved at a high pitch. The back wheels of the car almost lifted from the dirt road and she could hear the gravel spitting up behind her.

The silhouette of a man darkened the beam of one of her headlights. He was coming toward them. She wasn't going to let him stop her. She gave a quick glance in the rear view mirror. Ann's eyes were wide, but when Kimi quirked an eyebrow, she nodded.

Her hands clenched the wheel and then she released the brake. The car jumped forward just as a man was within yards of them. He jumped out of the way. The steering wheel bounced in her hands as she drove off the path onto the bushy terrain beside the road. She held the car straight.

The light from one of the trucks veered her way. She glanced to the side. It was a giant off-road vehicle with wheels as large as the car. It was headed straight at them. It was going to ram the side of the car and continue right over the top. There was no way they would survive.

She slammed on the brakes.

The truck flew past them.

She threw the car in reverse and then leaned over the back of her seat so she could navigate the vehicle. She swung it in a circle and then geared into drive. She gave the wheel a sharp turn to the right and was heading back to the main road.

The monster truck had left a space.

She steered for it.

The off-road vehicle that had tried to squish them was spinning back toward her. It was going to be too late. She kept the car on course. Within seconds, she had passed the vehicles that had kept them captive. The road, and freedom, was just ahead.

Out of nowhere, another set of lights blinded her. She steered away, but loss control on the rocky edge of the dirt track. The car spun around and came to a stop. The engine died. Her hands were shaking, but she wasn't giving up. She tried the key in the ignition and pumped the gas pedal.

It refused to start.

A man was walking toward them.

She grabbed the gun that Niail's had left, just as her door was pulled open. She aimed the pistol and pulled the trigger.

Nothing happened.

The safety was on. She could have cried with frustration. The weapon was wrenched from her hands, and she was yanked out of the car. He dragged her away from the vehicle and shook her.

"You bitch." The man's voice shouted at her. "It'll be a pleasure to kill you."

Kimi swung her legs out to kick her attacker. He held her at a distance so none of her blows hit him. She struggled to twist herself out of his grasp. He held tight. When she was panting from exhaustion, he gripped both of her arms around her waist and pulling her close to him. He chuckled close to her ear. His stale breath gagged her.

"You can't win. I'll..." His words stopped mid-sentence. She heard the sickening crunch of a bone breaking and then his hold on her arms slackened. She pulled free just as his body flew past her on the right. Another man stood before her. He was a giant.

"Are you hurt?" A familiar voice asked.

"Partlan?" Kimi sagged against the car hood. "When did you get here?"

"Just in time, I would say."

Partlan took her arm and led her to the passenger side. He opened the door and helped her into the seat. She sagged back against the head rest. Her body was shaking with the after effects of adrenaline and fear. Partlan went around the car and slid behind the steering wheel.

"Are you here alone?" Kimi hardly recognized her voice it was so weak.

"The others are with me."

"Niail is back there."

"We are aware." Partlan glanced over at her. "You and the children are our first priority. Niail knows this."

Kimi forced back a sob. She wanted to yell at him to save Niail, but she knew he would follow the code he lived by. A flicker of hope burned within her, though. There was a chance that Niail might live.

"Hold on." Partlan turned the key and the engine started.

He drove straight at the vehicles holding them captive. He came to within a few feet of them, and then slammed the brakes on. He opened the door and looked over at her.

"Get behind the wheel. Drive around the truck and leave if I don't return."

"Where are you going?" Kimi's voice shook.

"I need to remove the obstacles blocking your escape." Partlan shut the door and walked away.

"You had better do what he said." Ann's voice was calm, almost surreal from the rear seat. "I don't know who he is, but he's big enough to scare those guys into leaving."

Kimi giggled. It was a delayed reaction to all that was happening. It was inappropriate, but she couldn't help herself. Partlan would do what he said. Just like Niail was doing what he had promised her. He was protecting her and the children even if it meant he would die doing it. She scooted to the driver's side and started to rev the engine.

One by one the headlights went out.

Partlan had made escape possible.

She threw the car into drive and drove past the trucks. She stopped when Partlan appeared in her headlights. He came to the driver's window.

"We are going back for Niail. Go to your house and wait for us there."

"How will I know if he's safe?"

"You are his mate. Focus and you will know." Partlan moved away.

Chapter 21

'Stop.'

The word reverberated through Niail's head causing splinters of agony to shoot across his skull. When the pain lessened, relief coursed through him. It was his fellow Hunters speaking to him. He could hear his brothers through mind connect.

"What took you so long?" Niail spoke in a hoarse voice.

"We had to rescue your mate first." Partlan eased his hold on Niail. "She is safe."

"Good." Niail shook off the hands of Gur, Turlo, and Malac. "I heard your voices. It caused discomfort, but it is the first I have connected since my accident."

Partlan grunted. "You will heal fully. Now we must finish this. Here is another weapon."

Niail grabbed the assault rifle and checked the magazine. It was half full. Just then, an SUV with its headlights turned off, shot past them. He raised the rifle to shoot the tires, but Partlan motioned him to stop.

"We finish here first." Partlan threw a set of keys at Gur. "Follow him and wait for us to join you."

Partlan motioned to Turlo and Malac. "Niail, stay and shoot those who try to run. We're going at them from behind. We will move them to you."

Niail nodded. It was a familiar tactic for him. As the unit's sharpshooter he often stayed in place while his targets were driven within range. They would make short work of it here, and then move on to the SUV.

He balanced his rifle and popped up the front sight housing. He moved his neck and shoulders around to loosen them and then he settled behind the gun. He stared down the barrel and waited.

It took a few minutes, but eventually five men ran toward him. Each was firing a weapon. Niail took careful aim and hit all of his targets. He continued to hold his position until an '*all clear*' sounded in his head.

Malac reached him first. "Your aim was true as usual. You had already killed ten before we reached them."

"By Cygnus and Warrior, it is hard to kill a Hunter." Niail stood with his rifle resting on his folded arms.

"Now we follow their leader." Partlan started walking toward the road. The rest followed. The first truck they reached had no driver in sight. The keys were in the ignition and it was still running.

"This is the one that went after Kimi." Partlan climbed into the driver's seat. "He is dead now."

A surge of gratitude flooded Niail. Words were not needed to express his feelings. Turlo and Malac each slapped him on the back as they all climbed into the box of the truck.

They drove for several miles and then turned onto a paved road. Niail raised an eyebrow at Malac. "Has Gur found the other SUV?"

"Yes." Malac leaned forward. "It is Kowal. He has gone back to his warehouse."

Niail closed his eyes and tried to focus on mind connecting with Partlan, but it was useless. He had heard Partlan earlier, but his head was not fully healed. He tried to link with Kimi. He was more successful here. He could feel her as if she were right beside him. She was anxious, her heart was pounding, and her breathing was shallow.

He sent her a wave of calm. He sent her love and reassurance. Within seconds he felt her ease. He leaned back and savored the connection. The bond with his mate was growing stronger. Despite being unable to connect fully with his brothers, he could reach Kimi. She was safe.

They stopped on the road when they reached Kowal's warehouse. They each carried weapons as they walked to the building. Gur joined them in the parking lot.

"Another vehicle just came." Gur kept his voice low. "Ranon and the police officer went inside."

Partlan nodded. "Anybody else?"

"A group on motorcycles arrived five minutes earlier."

"They were inside before Ranon went in?" Partlan's voice was clipped.

"Yes." Gur motioned to the rear of the building. "There is an unlocked entrance there."

Partlan divided them. Gur, Turlo, and Malac went to the back of the warehouse. He and Partlan would go through the front entrance. Stealth was their main tool. Niail knew the mission. He crept alongside the building and waited for Partlan's command. They waited until the others were in the building before attempting the door.

It wasn't locked.

He followed Partlan inside. There were stairs on the side and Partlan motioned him up.

"Find a location to aim from. You will have our backs in case we need it." Partlan moved toward a set of closed double doors. "If you can mind connect, great. If not, follow the standard operating procedure."

Niail nodded and crept up the stairs. At each stair he paused to make sure the slight creak of the wood had not been heard. When he reached the top, he edged to the loft railing. He had a view of the whole warehouse from here.

There was an open half wall for about one third of the area. The rest was office space with windows that reached the rafters. The office area would make the best vantage point to shoot from. He eased a desk close to one of the open windows. Once his rifle was in position, he waited.

There were several men below. Jake and Ranon were

two of them. Ten men in motorcycle gear stood off to the side. They wore the orange colors of the FD Warriors. Their arms were crossed. Their eyes narrowed as they watched the other occupants of the warehouse. They were not pleased.

"This is a minor setback." A large man with a sagging midsection was saying from the center of a barricade of crates. "I'll have it taken care of now."

"You plan on killing every policeman that finds out about your dealings Kowal?" Jake was standing beside Ranon. "It can't be done."

"I don't have to kill them. Everybody has a price." The large man answered. Niail moved his rifle so that Kowal was in his scope.

"That's what you thought when you hired Hunters. All you did was anger them." Jake sounded as if he believed that Hunters existed. "Your only chance of survival is to be arrested."

A grunt of approval went up from the bikers at the side. "He's not wrong. We're out of this deal. There's no way we're taking on Hunters again."

The bikers started to move for the exit, but Kowal's voice stopped them. "You can't walk out. You're the reason that I hired them to begin with."

"You lied." The lead biker shook his head. "You have to deal with the consequences. If Hunters are protecting this reservation, then we won't do business here."

"There is no protection in place." Kowal cajoled. "I never took you guys for cowards."

"We're not fools." The lead biker pointed his finger at Kowal. "You've caused your own demise. You should have come to us before seeking out Hunters. We would have taken your territory, but you would have had your life. We have nothing further to discuss."

"Make sure I don't see you anywhere near this state,"

Jake yelled after them. "Otherwise, I'll haul your asses to jail too."

The group left. Niail watched them go with mixed feelings. They had not done any harm and they were leaving without a fight. The only honorable thing was to let them go. As long as they did not threaten the people here, there was no reason to pursue them.

Quiet descended on the warehouse. Ranon stepped forward. "The only one we have an argument with is Kowal. The rest of you have a chance to leave with your lives."

"I'm still arresting you." Jake frowned at Ranon. "This is a police investigation."

"We are not concerned with that." Ranon crossed his arms over his chest. "This is your last chance."

"Shoot them." Kowal barked the order.

Two of his guards raised their weapons and aimed. Before they could fire Niail had shot them both. They fell forward on the cement floor.

All hell broke loose then. Kowal ran for the exit and Niail took aim. Kowal ducked behind a crate before he could get a shot off. He focused on the rest of the men, but they had thrown their weapons away, and were lying face down on the hard floor.

That left Kowal.

There was no respite for him. Death was the justice that they would demand. He had broken his word and contract. He had tried to besmirch the honor of a Hunter. He would die for that.

"Come out." Jake walked toward where Kowal was hiding. "You will be protected by the police."

"I cannot promise that." Partlan came into the warehouse. "He has broken our code."

"That's all well and good for you guys, but here we follow the law." Jake kept moving toward Kowal. "You will have to let this one go."

Just then Kowal stood up. He had a gun in his hand and it was aimed at Jake. "I'm not going anywhere with you."

Jake hesitated a second, and that gave Kowal the opportunity he needed. From Niail's vantage point, he could see Kowal pull the trigger back. He took aim and shot the gun out of the man's hand. It went flying into the air. Niail's next shot was between Kowal's eyes.

The man fell down dead.

Jake shook his head and looked behind him. His eyes scanned the upper offices until he found Niail. He stared at him for a second and then turned back to the other men on the floor. He took a cellphone out of his pocket and began dialing.

"I'll have reinforcements here in a few minutes." Jake threw some handcuffs onto the ground. "If you guys wouldn't mind cuffing these ones, that'll make it easier for me to watch them while I wait. That is of course, if you don't have plans to kill them?"

"They did not contact us directly." Ranon picked up a set of cuffs and put them on the first man. "They're only guilty of obeying. I would suggest that they will continue to make poor choices despite your legal system."

"Are you joking?" Jake raised an eyebrow as Gur, Turlo and Malac entered from the back. "I never really stood a chance of getting Kowal alive?"

"It was a matter of honor." Partlan motioned Niail down from the loft. "We have to make certain Niail's mate is safe. She and the children were almost killed by Kowal's men tonight."

"What?" Jake pulled the phone from his ear. "Why didn't I hear about this?"

"You were more concerned in keeping the perpetrator alive." Partlan's gaze didn't leave Jake. "You would make a good warrior, but you need to understand a Hunter does not rest until he is finished."

Jake glared back at Niail. "Where were you when all this was happening?"

Niail's chest tightened. He understood Jake's anger. He had tried to keep Kimi safe and failed. The children had been exposed to a monster, and she had been forced to flee for their lives. They were alive, but at what cost. The only consolation he had was that Kowal would never threaten her or the children again.

"He protected his mate." Partlan's voice was harsh. "He sacrificed himself, so that she could escape."

Jake's shoulders seemed to sag. Niail hefted his rifle against his shoulder. He waited until Jake was finished with his phone call before approaching him.

"I did my best to protect Kimi and the children."

Jake nodded. "You also stopped Kowal from killing me."

"It is what we do." Niail looked over at Kowal's body. "He would never have stopped. A man like that can reach across any barrier."

"I believe that the law works." Jake's tone was defensive. "Otherwise, we would have everyone killing each other over some stupid argument."

"Perhaps." Niail sighed. "All I know is that even in the most enlightened society of our homeland, we were necessary."

Partlan came up to them. "We leave now."

Chapter 22

Kimi pulled up to her house. She shut the engine off and then dropped her head on the steering wheel. She had made it. She didn't know how, but somehow they were home.

Ann who had been silent, shifted in the rear seat. Wil and Peta had been huddled together on the floor the whole way. A blanket still covered them. Ann pulled the blanket off.

"We're home." Kimi didn't recognize her voice it was so hoarse.

"Is it safe?" Peta peered over the front seat.

"Yes." Ann opened the back door. "The sooner we're inside, the better we'll feel."

Kimi hoped so. Right now she didn't feel anything. Her body and brain were numb. Too much had happened in the last few days. All she could do was feel, and even that was hard to do.

The door of her house swung open.

Her heart started pounding.

Someone was there before them. Kowal had known all along that she would return home and had waited for her. She moved to turn the car back on, but Ann's hand on her shoulder stopped her.

"Look." Ann's voice was calm. "It's your grandfather."

Her shoulders sagged and she leaned her head against the back of the seat. A smile twisted her lips. Grandfather would know what was best. Kimi eased out of the car. Ann and the children scrambled into the house. Kimi followed them, giving her grandfather a hug on the way in.

"What happened?"

Kimi waited until the door was shut before speaking. "Kowal kidnapped Wil and Peta."

"He's a mean man." Wil tugged at Grandfather's shirt. "He threatened to hit us if we weren't quiet. It's okay now. Niail came."

A sob rose in Kimi's throat and she choked it back. Partlan had said she would know if Niail was safe. She felt nothing. It didn't seem possible that he would have been able to live through the barrage of bullets she had heard as she drove away from the clearing.

"Sit down Mommy." Peta took her hand and led her to a chair.

"How did you get here Grandfather?" Kimi tried to keep her voice calm. "You were with Jake."

"Your brother was determined to arrest Kowal." Grandfather sat beside her and took her hand in his. "The other Hunter went with him."

Kimi nodded. "Ranon. They must have gone into town. Kowal contacted us about a meeting place after you had left."

"When will Niail come back?" Wil asked.

"Soon." Ann hugged Wil. "I think we've had enough excitement for one night. It's bedtime."

Kimi came out of her reverie. She still had the children to consider, no matter what happened to Niail. She pushed back from the table and together she and Ann got the children to bed. When she was tucking Wil in, a sensation of love surrounded her. She almost fell over with the surge of adoration that hit her. She inhaled and then she knew.

Niail was alive.

Tears pricked her eyes. She didn't understand how it was possible, but just as Partlan had said, Niail had contacted her.

"Will Niail be here in the morning?" Wil's voice was hopeful. "I know he's a superhero, but even superheroes have to say goodbye."

Kimi kissed him on the forehead. "He'll be here when you wake up."

"I want to see him."

"When he gets here, I'll have him come and talk to you." Kimi placed Wil's teddy bear close to his cheek. "How would you like Grandfather to tell you a story?"

Wil nodded. "He will send any bad spirits away so I can sleep."

Kimi smiled. Wil trusted in her grandfather's medicine completely. The night's ordeal would fade for him once Wil had made certain that Niail was safe. Peta was another story.

Peta was huddled up at the top of her bed. Kimi almost cried at the look of fear in her daughter's eyes. She was only a year older than Wil, but it would take a long time before she healed from the night's terrors.

Kimi went up and sat beside her. She brushed her dark brown hair from her forehead. "Are you still frightened?"

"Is Niail dead?" Peta's voice trembled.

Kimi shook her head. "He is alive."

"You're certain?" Peta started to unfold her arms. "Those men were scary. They said that they wanted to kill Niail."

"Niail promised to protect us, and he did." Kimi folded Peta into her arms. "You don't have to be afraid anymore."

Peta relaxed into Kimi's embrace. Kimi rocked and soothed her with a soft lullaby until she heard Peta's soft even breathing. She had fallen asleep.

Kimi eased Peta back onto her pillows and pulled the covers up. Her daughter was exhausted. Later, they would deal with the trauma of the kidnapping. They would all need healing and that would take time. Her grandfather would know what to do.

She had felt Ann's eyes on her as she had settled the children for bed. She knew her friend disagreed with how she was dealing with the situation, but thankfully Ann waited until they had left the room before saying anything.

"How could you promise that?" Ann's voice was a harsh whisper. "There is no way Niail survived."

"I know he's alive." Kimi smiled. "Somehow, he is in my head and heart. He has sent me love and comfort."

Ann shook her head. "I hope so, or you're going to have hell to pay in the morning."

"He will be here." Kimi went into the kitchen and put the kettle on the stove. "Coffee?"

For the next half hour Kimi felt Niail's presence strengthen. It was almost as if his arms surrounded her. She hugged herself with the joy of knowing that he had been right. They had a bond that would only grow stronger.

They were just finishing their drinks when they heard vehicles pull up at the house. Every muscle in Kimi tensed. Then a wave of love and anticipation embraced her. It was Niail. She ran for the door.

It swung open before she could reach it. Partlan and the other Hunters walked in first. Then Niail stepped into the house. She threw herself into his arms. It took a second to realize he was covered in dried blood.

She pulled back and started to feel along his chest. "Are you hurt?"

"It is the blood of my enemy." His voice was gentle. "I did what was necessary to keep my promise to return to you."

He pulled her close and kissed her.

The world spun away.

All that existed was Niail. She gave herself to him heart and soul. She let him know by her kiss that she was his. She had always been his; she just hadn't known it until tonight. When the kiss ended she stared up at him. Her eyes devoured every precious inch of his face.

"I was so worried." Kimi's hands framed his face. "There were so many of them."

"I told you it was not easy to kill me."

Partlan cleared his throat. "I would also say that we arrived at the right time."

Niail kissed Kimi's forehead and then pulled her close. "That is why we work together. I am grateful you were able to save Kimi and the children."

"Yes, thank you Partlan." Kimi leaned closer to Niail. "Kowal's goon was too strong for me."

Grandfather came in from Wil's bedroom. He pulled out a chair beside him. "The children are safe and asleep. Sit and tell us the whole story."

Partlan took a seat, but the rest stood with their legs spread and arms crossed. Kimi leaned closer to Niail. He was alive, that was all she cared about. The details were inconsequential.

"Niail was out of ammunition when we reached him." Partlan grinned. "He was lucky his brothers had a weapon to give him."

Niail rubbed his chin against Kimi's head. "You were lucky I did not shoot you first."

"True. You gave us no choice but to tackle you." Malac shrugged. "You are weak."

"I have injuries." Niail's voice held amusement.

"A poor excuse." Malac's eyebrows rose. "Your head is not your only problem. Otherwise you would have heard your brothers' approach."

Kimi's heart lightened as she listened to the banter between these men. They might be warriors, but they had a bond that was indestructible. They didn't hide the fact that they watched over each other.

"My head is healing." Niail's fingers tightened on her waist. "I will be whole soon."

"This is good." Partlan leaned back in his chair. "We do not need to lose our best marksman."

Niail nodded and then looked at Grandfather. "Kowal is dead. Honor has been restored."

Grandfather sighed. "Jake?"

"He is the lawman still." Partlan's voice was gruff. "He wished to arrest Kowal, but the man raised his weapon to Jake. Niail ended it."

Kimi shivered. She was grateful that Jake was alive. She shuddered at the thought of what Niail had done to protect her family. It was horrific. She had always sought a peaceful resolution in every situation. Perhaps she should have tried harder, or chosen a different solution than running. But would it have changed things? Kowal was determined to hurt others.

Niail leaned close to her.

"This is not your concern. I will always protect you and your family." His words were a vow. "You need not worry about the means. That is for me to deal with."

Kimi glanced up at him. Somehow he had known her thoughts. The truth burned bright in his eyes. Their bond had strengthened, and it was more than she had thought possible.

"Some of Kowal's men surrendered." Partlan's voice held contempt. "Jake has taken them to jail. He will return when he has finished."

"The FD Warriors were also present." Malac shook his head. "They did not want to be involved once they knew that Kowal had dishonored us. They promised to leave the area."

"So there will be no more problems?" Ann spoke for the first time since the Hunters had arrived.

"You are all safe." Partlan crossed his arms. "The law may ask questions, but there should be no others coming for you."

Ann frowned and looked around the room. "Who are you, and what do I tell other people?"

"We were not there."

Ann pursed her lips. "Okay. So it was all a bad dream?"

"If you wish."

Ann pushed back from the table and took her mug to the sink. Kimi knew that she would have to do some serious talking with her friend about what had happened tonight, but that could wait. She moved away from Niail and touched her friend's arm.

"It will be fine."

Ann nodded. "I believe you. It will take a while for it to sink in."

Kimi pulled Ann close and hugged her. "Thank you for everything you did for the children. No one could have protected them more."

Ann's eyes misted up. "I'm just happy they're safe. I don't think I would have forgiven myself if they had been hurt."

"Will you forgive me for blaming you?"

"You were crazy with worry. It's forgotten." Ann sniffed and moved out of Kimi's reach. "It's time for me to go home."

Partlan stood. "Gur and Ranon will accompany you. They will make certain your house is safe."

The two stepped forward. Ann's eyes widened. She nodded and then handed the keys to Ranon. "I trust you can drive?"

"As you wish." Ranon opened the door and waited for Ann to pass through before turning to Partlan. "We will be on guard until we hear from you."

Partlan nodded. "It is best."

The room seemed bigger when the three of them had driven away. There were now only four Hunters in her small kitchen. Their large height and wide shoulders would stand out in any room. Their presence brought a sense of calm and security.

Kimi went to the table and started clearing up the mugs. She stopped beside her grandfather's chair. "You must be tired. Stay the night."

Her grandfather stood. "Jake has my truck."

"It's settled." Kimi put the mugs in the sink. "You can't wait for Jake to return. It could be hours."

She went to the room Niail had stayed in and changed the bedding. Her grandfather sat on the bed with a sigh. Kimi smiled and shut the door behind him. Now she had to find sleeping space for her other guests.

"I have the couches in the living room." Kimi gathered some more blankets. "Someone will have to sleep on the floor, though."

"It is not necessary." Partlan stood. "I will take first watch. Turlo and Malac will sleep first. Niail you will have last watch."

Niail nodded. Kimi didn't care which watch he was on. Right now he needed a shower and some clean clothes. The shower she could provide, the clothes might be a problem. She took his hand and led him to her bedroom.

"You can clean up in my bathroom." Kimi opened the adjoining door. "I'll hunt up some clothes."

Niail peeled off his shirt and then undid his jeans. Kimi felt the now familiar spark of desire twist through her. Delicious and intense; tonight she would sleep in Niail's arms and know she belonged there.

"You have decided to stay with me." Niail spoke in a husky voice. It was a statement, not a question.

"I knew the moment you left us in the car that I couldn't bear it if you died." Kimi reached for Niail's clothing. "I don't care what the future holds as long as you are by my side."

"I will never leave you."

Niail pulled off his briefs. He stood before her in all his glory. Kimi exhaled the breath she had been holding. A tendril of pleasure settled in her womb. This was her man; her mate. She gloried in being able to admit it.

She grabbed his briefs and went to the bedroom door. "I'll put these in the washing machine. There are clean towels near the shower."

She left the room and leaned against the closed door. She waited until her heart had stopped racing and then went to the laundry room. She put the clothes in for a soak and then scavenged through her cupboards looking for something that would fit Niail. She found a pair of jeans that Jake had left for mending and one shirt that was small, but would stretch. She went through the kitchen on her way to her room. Partlan stood there with his arms crossed. He was staring out the window and turned to look at her when she entered the room.

"Niail is a good man." His voice was gruff.

Kimi nodded. "I know."

"He is blessed to have found you." Partlan frowned. "With two Hunters having found mates, there is hope for the rest of us."

Kimi's gaze softened. These were such brave warriors. It was sinful that they had been denied the love and bond of a mate. She went over to him and put her hand on his arm.

"It will happen. No man should have to go through life alone."

"We have each other." Partlan cleared his throat. "Our brotherhood is important."

"Niail was devastated when he thought he had lost his connection with you." Kimi winced as she remembered Niail's pain when he had believed that he would never connect again. "He is healed now?"

Partlan nodded. "It will take more time before he is fully connected, but he is starting to hear us."

She sighed and started toward her bedroom. When she entered her bathroom the shower was still running. She put the clothes she had found on the counter and was about to leave when the shower door opened.

"Are you finished?" She reached for a towel.

"I am just starting." Niail captured her arm and pulled her into the shower. "Now I want to pleasure my mate."

Chapter 23

"In the shower?" Kimi giggled.

"Why not?" Niail nuzzled her neck. "It is invigorating and I need to be with you."

Kimi spread her hands over Niail's chest, savoring the feel of his beating heart. It pounded steady beneath her fingertips. It could have so easily been different. She leaned close and let her lips linger over his skin.

"You have too many clothes on."

Niail pulled her shirt over her head and made short work of the bra. He unzipped her jeans, but she had to help get them off her legs. Denim was impossible when wet. When she was naked he lifted her by the waist until she was positioned for him to enter her.

Her legs wrapped around him and in one swift movement he slid into her. She shuddered as a delicious tendril of pleasure spiraled through her. There was a sense of total oneness and belonging that was as erotic as the sensual rhythm Niail was creating with each thrust.

His teeth nibbled at her lips and then his tongue soothed her before Kimi opened for him. His tongue plunged in, sliding against hers and sending shivers of excitement through her veins. Together, they moved as one. It was fast and powerful as they built a tension of bliss that burst with an explosive shattering of ecstasy.

Their lips clung together as they descended the heights. Tiny shivers of sensation still skittered across Kimi's body. They were still joined, together and complete. It was as it should be. Gradually, Niail lowered her and they took turns washing each other.

Passion sizzled between them.

Their hunger had not been appeased.

Niail turned the water off and lifted her into his arms. He stepped out of the shower with her and grabbed a towel to wrap around them.

"You will get cold." Niail rubbed it over her back.

Kimi kissed his chin. "So will you."

"Not with you in my arms." Niail threw the towel to the floor.

"You should put me down." Kimi hugged him closer. "We can't stay like this forever."

"I intend to stay with you always." Niail set her on the bed before joining her.

"Don't forget the children will be awake early."

"I am taking last watch. I will be up for them." Niail pulled the blanket over them. "That means I can pleasure you all night and you can sleep in the morning."

"You're spoiling me." Kimi stretched her arms out to him.

"You are my mate." Niail's pushed a strand of wet hair from her face. "To love and protect you is all I want."

"Will you live here with me?" Kimi's voice was hesitant. "Or will we have to move?"

"Your home is where I will be." Niail's heated gaze sent a shiver of renewed hunger through her. "On my planet, it is the woman who makes those decisions."

"It won't interfere with your work if we live here?"

Niail shook his head. "My fellow Hunters understand that my first priority is you and the children."

Kimi sighed. "So I can continue to be with my people."

"Always."

Niail captured her mouth in a searing kiss and any further doubts she had were silenced. Their tongue danced together in a sensual duel until Kimi was lost to everything but the sensations Niail was creating within her.

His lips moved lower, caressing her neck and then her breasts. His fingers feathered across her skin, sending shards of pleasure throughout her body.

His tongue flickered across her nipple and a jolt of excitement stirred in her womb. His teeth nipped and then suckled until she squirmed with the mounting tension. He moved to the other breast and began his sensual torture again. His hand roamed lower and touched the moist heat of her inner core. His finger caressed as his mouth suckled. She splintered into a blinding climax within seconds.

Niail held her as she recovered and then he was moving over and in her. She groaned as he filled her. She would never tire of being connected to him. He set a leisurely pace, driving deep and withdrawing slowly, only to plunge again. Each thrust of his powerful body sent Kimi higher and higher until they reached the edge and shattered together.

Their breathing was ragged. Their hearts pounded in unison as they descended back to reality. Niail gathered Kimi close and rolled onto his side. They were still connected. Kimi nuzzled his neck and inhaled his scent.

"I love you." Her voice was a faint whisper.

"You are my mate." Niail's voice was gruff. "You are the only woman I will ever desire. There is nothing I will not do for you."

"What if I wish you to love me again?"

Niail thrust and Kimi felt his renewed hardness. She smiled. He was inexhaustible, but she couldn't resist. She pushed him onto his back and straddled his hips.

"This time, I set the pace."

The smell of bacon frying woke Kimi from a deep sleep. She stretched her arms over her head. She couldn't remember ever feeling this good before. Niail had made love to her until the early hours of the morning. She had been too exhausted to even notice when he had left to keep watch.

She pushed back the covers and made her way to the washroom. A quick shower and she was wide awake. It was time to face the day and the aftermath of last night.

Niail knew the moment Kimi entered the kitchen. Her essence wrapped around him. It made him whole. She had been sleeping peacefully when he had gone for his watch. He was filled with deep satisfaction and pride at knowing he had given her pleasure.

Jake and Eluwilussit were at the table. Peta was on Jake's lap and Wil was beside Niail. The children had woke up at the crack of dawn and had been with him while he stood watch. Now Wil wanted to help prepare breakfast. He stood on a chair beside the stove and watched Niail tend the bacon.

Partlan was leaning against the counter with a coffee in his hand. Turlo and Malac were beside the table talking to Eluwilussit.

"It's about time you woke up." Jake's voice boomed as Kimi entered the room. "You're the only one who had any sleep last night."

"Speak for yourself." Partlan grinned. "We sleep when we can."

Kimi went to the stove. "I'll finish."

Niail put his arm around her waist. "Did you sleep well?"

"You know I did." Kimi reached up and kissed his chin. "I didn't hear you leave for your watch."

"It was early." Niail smiled at Wil. "And I had company."

"I learned how to stand guard." Wil straightened his shoulders. "It's an important job."

Niail reached over and pulled Wil into his arms. "Your mother needs space to cook."

He took the chair over to the table and sat Wil on it. Kimi made short work of the eggs and toast, and within minutes everything was ready to go. Just then a vehicle pulled up outside.

Partlan pulled out a pistol and went to the door. Niail blocked the children with his body. Turlo and Malac stood in front of Kimi. Jake and her grandfather didn't have a chance to move before Partlan eased away from the door.

"It is safe." Partlan put his handgun back in the waistband of his pants. "It is Gur and Ranon returning with Ann."

The tension in the room eased. Kimi heaved a sigh and turned back to the stove. Once the newcomers were inside, she served breakfast. Afterwards, they stayed gathered in the kitchen.

"What are your plans?" Jake leaned back in his chair and looked at Niail.

"I will stay with Kimi."

"Just a second there buddy." Jake winked at his grandfather. "In the old days, a man would tie up horses outside the tipi of his father-in-law as payment for his wife.

"Hunters do not buy women." Partlan crossed his arms. "It is not honorable."

"But Kimi is Blackfeet," Jake continued. "She believes in living a traditional life."

Kimi leaned back into Niail's arms. "Women have freedom today."

"So you want to pick and choose what you believe and follow?" Jake shrugged. "I have no argument with that. It's what I do myself."

Kimi sighed. "You've made your point Jake."

Eluwilussit nodded. "Times change and we must keep abreast of what is new. Our people had difficulties when the buffalo disappeared, but we survived."

Ann, who was sitting next to Ranon, cleared her throat. Her eyes darted from Hunter to Hunter before settling on Eluwilussit. She put her coffee mug back on the table and straightened her shoulders.

"Do you know who these men are?"

"They are the ones who protect." Eluwilussit touched Ranon. "Can I see your symbols?"

Ranon looked over at Partlan, who nodded. He lifted his left sleeve. Ranon was clan Leigh which was symbolized by a circle and with an attached stick on one side.

Grandfather touched the clan symbol and nodded. "That is similar to the universal symbols given to us by the Star People. It is the spirit of doctoring."

Grandfather motioned Partlan over. He pointed to his arm.

"What is this symbol?"

"It is for clan Obair. We have the gift of the mechanical and instruments."

"For us it signifies the law of light, sound, and vibration. These are all parts of engineering."

"What does the fact that they wear these signs mean?" Ann asked in a hesitant voice.

"They carry the symbols of the universal laws that were given to us by the Star People." Eluwilussit looked at the men in the room. "I believe that they were sent to us for a reason."

"The Star People sent them?" Jake rolled his eyes. "That makes them aliens. They may be larger than most men, but they look human."

"I agree."

Silence followed Eluwilussit's announcement.

Kimi was the first to speak. "What are you suggesting?"

"There are many legends surrounding the Star People. All I know for certain is that they wear the symbols given to us. These men must have some connection with the people who visited earth from the stars."

"That may be why we were sent to this planet to be executed." Niail frowned. "It might also explain why Gur and Turlo were stranded here as children."

"So there is a connection between Cygnus and Earth?" Partlan's voice held doubt. "Why have we not heard of this before?"

Malac leaned back against the counter. "There is no mention of Earth in our histories. We know that we were not from Cygnus originally. The Ancients brought us from an inferior planet. We were bred and genetically modified to be elite warriors."

"So it's possible that inferior planet was Earth?" Jake laughed. "That's just a bit farfetched."

Niail sensed Kimi's fear. He sent her soothing thoughts.

"They may look human, but they have powers we don't." Kimi's voice shook. "The government would capture them if they knew this. No one can know about Niail or the others."

"It's too dangerous." Ann agreed. "I won't say a word. You guys saved my life."

"I'm not going to tell anyone. That will just ruin the story I told my bosses about last night." Jake snapped. "I'm not a fool."

Kimi exhaled. "Thank you. We have to make certain that this stays among us. Otherwise they will never be safe."

"What about a secret identity. All superheroes have one." Wil looked up from the picture he had been coloring. "Niail could be a football player."

Niail frowned. "What is football?"

"It's a sport." Kimi shook her head. "We have to choose something you know about."

"We know battle" Gur and Turlo spoke together.

"I know machines." Partlan added this.

"I know our history." Malac's voice was almost apologetic.

"I know medicine." Ranon smiled. "Our leader Ardal knows strategy, and Niail is the best marksman in the unit."

"So you guys could start and finish a war." Jake rolled his eyes. "That's not much of a cover."

"We could say they're ex-military, former members of your unit, Jake." Kimi bit her lip. "That way they wouldn't be noticed when they visit. Maybe we could add that they are running a private security firm now."

Jake shrugged. "It might work. These guys are noticeable where ever they go, but I doubt many on the reservation will question them once they know they're connected to our family."

"We already have a business; aHunter4Hire." Partlan crossed his arms. "We search for what is missing, and right what is wrong."

"Sounds like a security firm to me." Jake's voice was nonchalant. "No need to go into particulars, or what you call yourselves. While you're here, you're just ordinary citizens running a private enterprise."

"This will keep us safe?" Niail's voice was doubtful. Hiding had been the only choice since they had crashed on Earth.

"It's a reasonable story. People won't dig too deeply." Jake stood, lifting Peta onto the chair he had just vacated.

"It's time I headed back to the office. I have a very lengthy report to write. It seems the paperwork goes up exponentially as the number of bodies increase."

Jake gave Kimi a quick kiss and ruffled Wil's hair. "Ann could you give me a lift into town. I'll use one of the official cars until mine is fixed."

"No problem." Ann and Jake left together.

Eluwilussit cleared his throat. "I have two vehicles that need tires at my sweat lodge. Perhaps you fellows could help fix them?"

"We will drive our vehicle and follow you to get the tires." Partlan motioned to the others. "Once the tires are replaced we will return the vehicles."

"I would appreciate that." Kimi smiled at Partlan. "I'm loss without my truck."

Niail started to move with the other Hunters, but Partlan shook his head. "You are to stay here so that you can rest and heal."

"I can help."

"You are to follow your orders." Partlan held the door open for Eluwilussit. *'Ardal wants you with your mate. There is another assignment in California. If your help is needed we will contact you.'*

Niail grinned. He had heard Partlan clearly. He was connected again. He was one with his fellow Hunters; no longer alone.

When everyone had left Kimi turned to him. "Will you truly be safe?"

Niail hugged her close. "No one knows about our involvement with the shooting. Jake has made everything look as if it was something that he orchestrated."

"So there will be no questions?"

"None." Niail looked down into her eyes. "My concern is for Wil and Peta. That was a horrible ordeal for them."

Peta looked up from her drawing. "Wil and I knew that you would save us. That's what Hunters do."

Niail released Kimi and pulled a chair up between the kids.

"You were not afraid?"

Wil shook his head. "Not once you were there. We did what you told us and hid our heads. It was a bumpy ride. I don't think Mom is used to driving on the gravel roads."

"Grandfather says that we were protected." Peta picked up a blue crayon.

"We have strong medicine around us." Wil grinned at Niail. "That's why that mean man couldn't hurt us."

Niail looked up at Kimi. He had wanted the children to be spared the violence and fear that surrounded their kidnapping. Their trust in him had kept them safe. Time would tell if they had any lasting effects. He knew Kimi would be alert for that.

"Are you going to live with us now?"

"Would you like that?"

Both Wil and Peta nodded.

"It's cool having a superhero for a friend."

Kimi sat at the table and took both of the children's hands in hers. "What about having one for a father?"

Wil looked at Niail. "Are you going to marry Mom?"

"If your mother wishes, yes." Niail's eyes never left Kimi as he spoke. "I have bonded with your mother. There will never be any other woman for me."

"Does that include us?" Peta's hands were clasped together on the table.

Niail put his hand over hers. "We do not have children. It would be an honor if you would let me be a father to you."

"Why can't you have kids?" Wil tilted his head at him.

"Hunters are not allowed to have families. Where I come from children are not born. They are created in birthing chambers."

"Sounds icky." Wil wrinkled his nose. "I think it's easier if we become your children."

"So do I." Peta's voice was fierce. "What can we tell our friends?"

"That your Mom has fallen in love and is getting married." Kimi reached over to join hands with Niail. "They don't need to know anything else."

"Okay." Peta pushed her drawing away. "Can we go outside now?"

Kimi nodded. "Don't go far."

Wil and Peta raced for the door, banging it shut behind them. All that existed was Kimi now. Her love and care had saved his life. Her trust, made him strong. She had given him more than he had dreamt possible. She was his mate, and her children, his family.

He was drowning in her. He remembered the first time he had stared into her beautiful, brown eyes. He had thought he had lost everything, but it had been his salvation. He was a Hunter and Kimi was his mate. As long as she was by his side, he would always know who he was and where he belonged.

Author's Note

I have lived and taught on Reserve, and have a deep respect for Native Americans, their traditions and teachings. There are many legends among various North American tribes concerning people or beings from the stars. These legends include abductions, visitations, and ancestors who were extraterrestrials.

The symbols mentioned in the novel refer to the twenty-two universal and spiritual laws which are said to be observed by Star People throughout the universe.

Thank you for purchasing my book. I hope you enjoyed reading about the Hunters.

About the Author

Cynthia spent most of her childhood with her nose in a book. She began writing stories in her teens, but it wasn't until her forties that she took her writing seriously. Cynthia has an eclectic range of interests that includes reading, ghost hunting, exploring paranormal phenomena, history, quilting, gardening, and great conversation. She has a BSc in Biology, a BA in anthropology, and recently graduated from nursing. Cynthia enjoys writing the type of books she reads.

She writes romances where time and space meet love and honor. She lives in Northern Ontario with her husband of thirty years, her teenage son, and their two dachshunds.

If you would like more information about upcoming releases or Cynthia's other books, please visit her website at: www.cynthiaclement.com

Additional aHunter4Hire Books

aHunter4Rescue (Book 1)

aHunter4Life (Book 3)

aHunter4Ever (Book 4)